ILLUSTRATED CLASSICS

Heidi

Johanna Spyri

Adapted by
Lucy Collins

Edited by
Claire Black

Published by

Berryland
Books
www.berrylandbooks.com

Heidi

Johanna Spyri

First Published in 2006 • Copyright © Berryland Books 2006
ISBN 1-84577-092-7 • Printed in India

Contents

CHAPTER I

Alm Uncle

On a sunny morning in June two figures could be seen climbing the narrow mountain path from the village of Mayenfield in the Swiss Alps. One, a tall, strong looking girl; the other, was a small child not more than five years old. The child's little cheeks burnt crimson with the heat. This was nothing surprising, for in spite of the hot

June sun the child was clothed as if to keep off the bitterest cold.

When the two reached the hamlet of Dorfli, situated half-way up the mountain, a voice called to the tall girl from one of the scattered houses: "Wait a moment, Dete; if you are going up higher, I will come with you."

The girl addressed as Dete stood still, and the child immediately sat down on the ground.

"Are you tired, Heidi?" asked Dete.

"No, I am hot," answered the child.

"We shall soon get to the top now," said Dete encouragingly. "You must walk bravely on a little longer."

They were now joined by a stout, good-natured-looking woman who walked on ahead with Dete, while the child wandered behind them.

"And where are you off to with the child?" asked the newcomer. "I suppose it is the child your sister left?"

"Yes," answered Dete, "I am taking Heidi up to Uncle, where she must stay."

"The child stay up there with Alm Uncle!" exclaimed her companion. "You must be out of your senses, Dete! How can you think of such a thing! Anyway, the old man will soon send you and Heidi packing off home again!"

"No, he won't do that, Barbel," replied Dete. "He is her grandfather. He must do something for her. I have had the charge of Heidi till now, and I am not going to give up a golden opportunity for her sake."

"Where are you going?" asked Barbel.

"To Frankfurt," replied Dete. "After mother died last year, I went down to the Baths and found work there, entrusting Heidi to the care of old Ursel in the village. Now, the family I work for has asked me to go to Frankfurt with them. It's an excellent chance for me."

"Well, I am glad that I am not the child," said Barbel. "Everyone down here is terrified of

Alm Uncle with his bushy grey eyebrows and huge beard. He does not talk to anybody nor does he attend Church. And when he comes down the mountain carrying his big stick, everybody clears out of the way of him."

"Well, he is not likely to harm Heidi," snapped Dete, "and if he does, he will be answerable for it, not I."

"I would like to know," continued Barbel, inquiringly, "why does Alm Uncle live up there on the mountain like a hermit? All kinds of things are said about him. One doesn't know what to believe! You must certainly have learnt a good deal about him from your sister?"

"Yes, I did. But I am not going to repeat it; or I might get into trouble."

"You can tell me," coaxed Barbel, putting her arm confidentially through Dete's.

"All right!" agreed Dete. "But, wait a moment; where is Heidi?"

Dete stood still and looked all about her.

4

But she couldn't see the child anywhere.

"I see where she is," exclaimed Barbel. "Look over there!" and she pointed to a spot far away from the footpath. "She is climbing up the slope there with Peter the goatherd and his goats. Don't worry. She'll be all right. Now tell me about Alm Uncle."

"Uncle once owned the largest farm in Domleschg," began Dete. "He was the elder of two brothers. The younger brother was very orderly; but the elder fell into bad company and drank and gambled away the whole of his property. When his parents found out, they died of broken hearts."

"The younger brother, who had also become penniless now, went away in anger, and Alm Uncle too disappeared. Some say he went away to Naples and became a soldier. Nothing was heard of him for twelve or fifteen years. After that he returned to Domleschg with his little boy. His wife had died soon after their marriage. But he had earned such a bad name for himself in the village that every door was shut in his face."

"He then came to Dorfli with his son, who was called Tobias. Everybody liked Tobias. However, people still looked upon the old man with suspicion. Still, we did not refuse to acknowledge our relationship with Alm Uncle."

"And what happened to Tobias?" asked Barbel.

"Tobias learnt carpentry and soon got work in Dorfli. Then he married a girl from the village - my sister Adelaide. They had a little girl whom they also named Adelaide - but everyone called her Heidi. But misfortune struck the family and Tobias was killed in an accident. Adelaide never got over the shock. She developed a fever and died just two months later. People said it was punishment for Uncle's godless way of life. Some even went and told him so to his face! After that, Uncle became more bitter then ever and stopped talking to everyone. And one day, he went to live alone up the Alm intending never to come down again."

"Little Heidi came to live with me and my mother. And since mother's death I have cared for her alone."

"And you are going to give the child over to the old man up there?" exclaimed Barbel. "I am surprised that you can even think of doing such a thing!"

"What do you mean?" said Dete. "I can't take a five years old child with me to Frankfurt! Anyway, tell me Barbel, where are you going to yourself? We are now halfway up the Alm!"

"We have just reached my destination," answered Barbel. "I have something to say to the goatherd's wife."

And Barbel bid Dete goodbye and went towards a small hut.

The old hut was so broken-down that it was quite unsafe for living in. When stormy winds came sweeping over the mountain, everything inside the hut shook and rattled; and all the rotten old beams creaked and trembled.

Eleven year old Peter lived here. Every morning, Peter went down to Dorfli to fetch the goats and drive them up on to the mountain. The goats grazed till evening on the delicious mountain plants. In the evening, Peter would return with the goats to Dorfli and hand them over to their owners. Then he would play with the children for some time before returning home to a supper of bread and milk.

Peter stayed with his mother and blind grandmother. His father had died a few years before.

Dete stood for quite some time looking about her for the children and the goats. However, they were nowhere to be seen.

Meanwhile, the two children were climbing up the mountain by a far and roundabout way, for Peter knew many spots where all kinds of good shrubs and plants grew for his goats. Heidi, exhausted with the heat and weight of her thick covering of clothes, panted and struggled after Peter. She kept watching Peter, who jumped lightly here and there on his bare feet, dressed only in his short light breeches. Suddenly, Heidi sat down on the ground, and took off her shoes and stockings. Next, she threw away her red shawl and the two frocks which Dete had put one over the other to save herself the trouble of carrying them, and put them in a tidy heap on the mountain slope. Then, wearing only her thin sleeveless dress, she went away jumping happily with Peter and his goats.

Soon, the children came up to the cottage. No sooner did Dete see Heidi climbing up towards her, than she cried out, "Heidi, what have you been doing! Where are your two frocks and the red shawl? And the new shoes I bought?"

Heidi quietly pointed to a spot below on the mountain side and answered, "Down there."

"What!" exclaimed Dete, angrily, "Why have you done that?"

"I don't want them any more," Heidi answered.

Hearing this, Dete became furious.

"You thoughtless, good for nothing child," she scolded. "Have you no sense at all?"

Then she asked Peter to fetch Heidi's clothes, promising him something nice for his effort. Peter immediately ran down the mountain, as swift as a goat, and soon returned with the clothes. And when Dete handed him a coin, Peter promptly thrust it into his pocket and his face beamed with delight. It was not often that Peter was the happy owner of such riches.

After climbing for about an hour more, Dete and Heidi reached the wooden hut where Alm Uncle lived.

CHAPTER 2

Grandfather's Cottage

Alm Uncle's hut stood on a part of the mountain, from where a full view could be had of the valley below. Behind the hut, stood three old fir trees, and beyond these, was a further wall of mountain. The lower heights of the mountain were overgrown with beautiful grass and plants. Above these were stonier slopes that led gradually up to the steep, bare rocky peaks.

Outside the hut, on the side looking towards the valley, Uncle had put up a bench. Alm Uncle was sitting on this bench with his pipe in mouth.

Heidi went up to him, put out her hand, and said, "Good evening, grandfather."

The old man gazed long and searchingly at Heidi.

"So, what is the meaning of this?" he asked gruffly, as he gave the child a hasty shake of the hand.

Heidi too stared back at him in return. To her, the grandfather, with his long beard and thick grey eyebrows that looked just like a bush, seemed so remarkable looking, that she was unable to take her eyes off him.

"Good morning Uncle, I have brought you Tobias' and Adelaide's child," Dete told him.

"What's that?" the old man looked up. "What has a child to do with me?" he asked.

"The child is here to stay with you. I have done my duty and now it's your turn. If you cannot keep her with you, do as you like with her. Just remember that you are already called a bad man by many. So it is you who will have to answer if any harm falls on her," Dete rattled off.

Alm Uncle was so angry to hear this that he ordered Dete to leave the child and go away at once. Dete too, looking at Uncle's angry face, said goodbye to Heidi and quickly ran down the hill. She knew what she was doing wasn't right as Heidi had been left in her care by her dying mother. She was thus going away with an uneasy conscience.

As soon as Dete had left, the old man went back to his bench and sat down without saying anything. In the meantime, Heidi went around the cottage, looked at the surroundings, peeped inside the goat-shed and finally returned to where Alm Uncle was sitting. She stood before the old man and gazed at him.

"What do you want to do?" asked Alm Uncle.

"I want to see what you have inside the cottage," said Heidi.

"Come then." And Alm Uncle rose and went before her towards the hut. "Bring your bundle of clothes in with you."

Heidi did as she was told. The old man now opened the door and the child stepped inside after him. Heidi looked around and saw that it was quite a large room. There was a table, and a chair, and in one corner stood Alm Uncle's bed. In another corner was the fireside with a large kettle hanging above it. There was also a big door in the wall; this was the cupboard. Alm Uncle opened it. Inside, lying on a shelf, were his clothes. On a second shelf there were some plates, cups and glasses. On another shelf there was a round loaf, smoked meat, and cheese.

Heidi shoved her bundle of clothes inside the cupboard.

"Where am I going to sleep, grandfather?" Heidi wanted to know.

"Wherever you wish," grandfather replied.

Heidi at once started examining the room to find out where it would be nicest to sleep. Then she saw a ladder in the corner. She climbed up and found herself in the hayloft. Inside, there was a large heap of fresh sweet-smelling hay. In the wall was a little round window through which she could see right down the valley.

"I shall sleep up here, grandfather," she called down to him, "It's lovely up here. Come up and see how lovely it is!"

"Oh, I know all about it," grandfather told her.

"I am getting the bed ready now. But I want you to bring me up a sheet," Heidi instructed. "You can't have a bed without a bed-sheet."

"All right," said grandfather.

But, as he did not have any sheets, he found Heidi some pieces of hard cloth. They made an excellent bed-sheet for her bed. Meanwhile, Heidi had put some extra hay at one end for a pillow. Then, the two together spread the sheet over the hay bed. Now the bed looked very tidy and comfortable indeed.

However, Heidi was gazing thoughtfully at their work.

"We have forgotten something, grandfather," she cried.

"What's that?" grandfather asked.

"A coverlet; when you get into bed, you have to creep in between the sheets and the coverlet."

Then grandfather searched up a large and thick flax sack and spread it over Heidi's bed. It made a splendid coverlet.

"It's lovely," declared Heidi. "I wish it was night, so that I might get inside it at once."

"I think we should get us something to eat, first," said grandfather. "What do you think?"

In her excitement Heidi had quite forgotten that she was very hungry!

"Yes, I think so too," she replied.

So, the two of them went down the ladder. Grandfather took out a large piece of cheese and held it on a long iron fork over the fire. He turned it round and round till it was toasted a nice golden yellow color on each side. Heidi watched everything eagerly and curiously. Then, remembering something, she ran towards the cupboard. She got out the bread, two plates and bowls and arranged them on the table.

"Good!" said grandfather, "It looks like you can think for yourself."

Heidi dragged a three legged stool from the fire-side and sat down on it. But the table was too high for her. So, grandfather put her plate and bowl on his chair, and himself had his lunch sitting on the table.

They ate bread and delicious roasted cheese. Heidi lifted the bowl of goat's milk with both hands and drank without pause till it was empty.

"I never drank such good milk before," said she.

Hearing this, grandfather filled up her bowl again.

After they had finished their meal, grandfather went outside to the goat shed. He swept it out and put fresh straw for the goats to sleep upon. Then he went to the tool-shed and made a high chair for Heidi so that she could easily reach the table.

Heidi followed him everywhere, watching attentively all that he did. Everything that she saw was a fresh source of delight to her.

Soon, it was evening. The wind began to roar loudly through the old fir trees. Heidi listened with delight to the sound, and it made her so happy that she skipped and danced round the old trees.

Suddenly, a shrill whistle was heard. It was Peter, coming down the heights with the goats. From among the flock, two goats came towards grandfather. One was white and the other brown in color. They began licking grandfather's hands as he had always a little salt ready for them when they returned.

Peter, meanwhile, left with the remainder of his flock.

"Oh, they are so pretty!" exclaimed Heidi, tenderly stroking the two goats one after another. "Are they ours, grandfather? Will they stay with us?" she asked.

"Yes, yes," grandfather convinced her. "Now eat your supper."

He milked the white goat which was called Little Swan and filled up Heidi's bowl. The brown goat was called Little Bear.

Heidi had her bread and milk and said

goodnight to grandfather. She also said goodnight to Little Swan and Little Bear and happily skipped off to bed.

Soon, Heidi was lying on her hay bed as sweetly and soundly asleep as any young princess on her couch of silk.

During the night such a stormy wind started blowing that the hut trembled, and the old beams groaned and creaked. Grandfather got up in the middle of the night. "Heidi will be frightened," he murmured. He climbed the ladder and went and stood by the child's bed.

The moonlight was falling through the round window straight on to Heidi's bed. She lay under the heavy coverlid, with a happy expression on her baby face as if dreaming of something pleasant. Grandfather stood looking down on the sleeping child for some time; then he went back to bed.

CHAPTER 3

Up on the Mountain

Heidi was woken up early the next morning by the sound of a loud whistle. It was Peter calling his goats. Heidi dressed quickly and climbed down.

"Would you like to go with Little Swan and Little Bear up the mountain?" asked her grandfather.

"Yes, yes," Heidi was overjoyed.

"But you must first wash and make yourself tidy. Otherwise the sun that shines so brightly will laugh at you for being dirty. See, I have put everything ready for you."

Her grandfather pointed to a large tub full of water, which stood in the sun before the door.

Heidi ran to it and began splashing and rubbing.

Meanwhile, grandfather packed a large piece of cheese and bread for Heidi and gave them to Peter. Peter's eyes went wide on seeing such a large size of cheese. It was twice as large as the one he had for dinner! Then grandfather gave him Heidi's bowl and said, "Milk one of the goats for her."

Heidi now came running in.

"Will the sun laugh at me now, grandfather?" she asked anxiously.

Grandfather saw that Heidi had rubbed herself so thoroughly that she had become as red as a lobster. He gave a little laugh.

"No, there is nothing for the sun to laugh at now," he assured her.

Then the two children set off up the mountain along with the goats.

The bright sun was shining down on the green slopes of the mountain that were covered with brightly-colored flowers. Heidi ran here and there shouting with delight. She plucked whole handfuls of the flowers and put them into her little apron. She wanted to take them all home and stick them in the hay, so that she might make her bedroom look just like the meadows outside.

On the other hand, Peter was having a hard time looking after both Heidi as well as the goats that were as lively as the little girl.

"Come along here!" he called. "Or you will fall over the rocks. Your grandfather told me to see that you don't."

"Where are the rocks?" asked Heidi.

"Right up above. And on the topmost peak the great old hunter bird sits and croaks."

Hearing this, Heidi immediately jumped up and ran to Peter. Then they began climbing higher up the mountain.

Soon, they reached the place where Peter usually took the goats for grazing. Peter took off his wallet and put it carefully in a little hollow of the ground so that it would not blow away. He was quite tired after the long climb and soon lay on the ground and fell fast asleep. Heidi too sat down beside Peter and looked about her.

"Peter, Peter, wake up!" called out Heidi after a while. "See, the great hunter bird is there look, look!"

Peter sat up.

Together, they sat and watched the bird which rose higher and higher in the air till it disappeared behind the grey mountain-tops. Then Peter opened his wallet, took out the bread and cheese and called out to Heidi.

"It is time for lunch," said Peter. "Sit down now and begin."

He filled up Heidi's bowl with fresh milk and then took out his own food. Heidi took up her bowl and drank the milk. Then she broke off a piece of her bread and gave the remaining piece, along with the whole big slice of cheese to Peter.

"You can have that, I have plenty," Heidi said.

Peter was so amazed that he was unable to speak and just stared at Heidi. He could not believe that Heidi really meant to give him her portion of bread and cheese. At last, when he saw that she really meant it, he took the food and nodded his thanks. He had never had a more splendid meal before!

"Tell me the names of all the goats Peter," said Heidi.

Peter knew all their names by heart. So, he told Heidi the names of all the goats. Heidi listened very carefully, and soon she could call each goat by name.

"Why does little Snowflake cry so?" Heidi wanted to know.

"Because she misses her mother," informed Peter.

Heidi hugged the young animal. "Poor Snowflake!" she cried. "Do not cry. I shall come here with you every day."

Snowflake rubbed her head against Heidi's shoulder, and stopped crying.

Soon, it was afternoon. Suddenly, Heidi jumped to her feet, "Peter! Peter! Everything is on fire! All the rocks are burning, and the great snow mountain, and sky!"

"It is always like that," Peter said calmly; "but it is not really fire."

"What is it then?" cried Heidi, as she ran backwards and forwards to observe it from all sides.

"It becomes like that by itself," explained Peter.

"O how beautiful! Look at the crimson snow! Oh! Now they are turning grey! Now all the colors are gone, Peter."

And Heidi sat down on the ground looking distressed.

"It will come again tomorrow," Peter told her. "Get up, we must go home now."

On returning home, Heidi asked, "Why does the great bird croak and scream so, grandfather?"

"First go and get into your bath while I get some milk. When we sit down for supper, I will tell you all about it."

Heidi obeyed. And later, when she was sitting on her high stool before her milk bowl, she repeated her question, "Why does the great bird go on croaking at us, grandfather?"

"He is mocking the people who live down below in the villages, because they gossip and quarrel," said grandfather.

Then Heidi told him about all the

wonderful things she had seen on the mountain and the great fire. Heidi wanted to know how it all had happened for Peter knew nothing about it. Grandfather explained to her that it was the sun that did it: "When he says goodnight to the mountains he throws his most beautiful colors over them, so that they may not forget him before he comes again the next day."

Heidi was delighted with this explanation.

That night, she dreamt of the mountains and little Snowflake running about.

CHAPTER 4

A Visit to Grandmother

Every day, Heidi went with Peter and the goats. Day by day she became browner, and grew so strong and healthy that she was never ill. Then autumn came, and the wind blew louder and stronger. On the days it was extremely windy, grandfather would say, "Today, you must stay at home, Heidi. The mighty wind would blow a little thing like you over the rocks into the valley down below!"

So, Heidi would stay at home and watch her grandfather make cheese, and sometimes do carpentry. On such days, Peter and even the goats became unhappy as they had to go without Heidi.

Then, gradually, it grew very cold. So, Heidi went to the cupboard and got out her shoes and stockings and dress. Soon, Peter stopped coming, as one night there was a heavy snowfall and the whole mountain was covered with it. Thick snowflakes kept falling till the snow was up to the window of the cottage. Then the snow grew so high that the window could not be opened.

One day, Peter came to visit them, covered all over with snow.

"Well, general," said grandfather, "now that you have lost your army, you will have to turn to your pen and pencil."

"Why must he turn to his pen and pencil?"

asked Heidi.

"During the winter he must go to school," explained grandfather, "and learn how to read and write."

Then grandfather asked Peter to join them for supper, and the three of them sat down to a meal of bread, butter and roasted meat.

Peter enjoyed the meal very much.

Before going home Peter said, "Grandmother wants you to come and see her someday, Heidi."

It was quite a new idea to Heidi that she should pay anybody a visit. So, the first thing she said to her grandfather the next day was, "I must go down to see grandmother today."

"Not today," said grandfather. "The snow is too deep."

But Heidi had made up her mind to go, since grandmother had sent her that message. So, she reminded her grandfather that she had to go to see grandmother, five or six times each day! On the fourth day, the snow had frozen into ice. Heidi again repeated her little speech, "I must certainly go down to see grandmother today."

This time, grandfather rose up, brought down Heidi's thick, sack coverlet, and said, "Come along then!"

Heidi skipped out happily after him into the sparkling world of snow. Grandfather got out his sleigh, and wrapping up Heidi in the coverlet, seated her inside. After that he himself got inside the sleigh and gave it a push. The sleigh went flying through the air like a bird.

Soon, they were at Peter's cottage. Her grandfather lifted Heidi out of the sleigh and told her to return home when it started getting dark. Then he again went up the mountain, pulling his sleigh after him.

Heidi opened the door of the little hut and found herself in a small room. An old woman was spinning in a corner of the room. Heidi was sure that this was grandmother. She went up to her and touched her shoulder, "Good-morning, grandmother. I have come to see you."

Grandmother lifted up her head and slowly took Heidi's hand.

"Are you the child who lives with Alm Uncle?" she asked.

"Yes, grandfather brought me here in his sleigh."

"What! Brigitta is it possible that Alm Uncle himself brought her here?" exclaimed grandmother.

Peter's mother had approached Heidi and was looking at her curiously.

"Probably the child is mistaken, mother," she said.

"I know quite well it was grandfather who brought me down in the sleigh," asserted Heidi.

"What Peter told us about Alm Uncle during the summer was true then! What is the child like, Brigitta?" grandmother asked Peter's mother.

"She is slim like Adelaide," said Brigitta. "But her eyes are dark and her hair is curly, like her father's and the old man's."

Meanwhile, Heidi was looking around the room. "Look grandmother," she cried, "one of your window shutters is flapping backwards and forwards!"

"Ah child, I can't see it," said the old woman. "But everything in the cottage rattles and creaks when the wind is blowing. Some nights I lie awake waiting for the house to fall down around us."

"Why can't you see the shutter, grandmother?" Heidi wanted to know.

"Ah, child, it is not only the shutter that I can't see - I can see nothing at all."

When grandmother explained to her that she would never see anything again, Heidi was filled with distress and began to cry.

"Can no one make you see again?" she sobbed.

Now grandmother tried to comfort Heidi, but it was not easy to quiet her. At last she said, "Come here, dear Heidi, let me tell you something. When a person can no longer see, even listening to a kind word brings much gladness. So come and sit beside me and tell me about your grandfather. I knew him very well in old days; but for many years now I have heard nothing of him. You see, Peter never says much."

So, Heidi quickly wiped away her tears and started talking of her life with grandfather. She also told grandmother about all the beautiful things that grandfather had made for her out of pieces of wood.

The old woman listened with great interest.

"Do you hear this, Brigitta?" she said. "Alm Uncle is kind to the child."

The conversation was interrupted by Peter marching in.

"Back from school already?" said his grandmother. "How quickly did the afternoon go by today! How's the reading getting on, Peter?"

"Just the same," replied Peter.

The old woman sighed. "I was hoping he'd have learned to read the old prayer-book with beautiful songs. I haven't heard them from a long time, and I can't even remember them any more."

The afternoon had grown darker and Heidi realized it was time for her to leave.

"Goodnight, grandmother, I must go home now," she said.

Then, bidding goodbye to Peter and his mother Heidi went towards the door.

"Wait," said the old woman. "You must not go alone! Peter must go with you."

But Heidi was already outside.

"Run after her, Brigitta," cried grandmother, "the child will be frozen to death on such a cold night as this; take my shawl, run quickly!"

Brigitta ran out. But she was surprised to see that Heidi's grandfather had come to meet her. He wrapped Heidi up in the sack and lifted her into his arms. Then, he started walking up the mountain.

Brigitta returned to the hut and told the grandmother everything she had seen. Grandmother was delighted to hear that Alm Uncle was so kind to little Heidi.

Meanwhile, Heidi was chattering away to her grandfather from inside her sack. However, her voice could not be heard properly through the many thick folds of her wrap.

"Wait till we get home," grandfather told her, "and then you can tell me all about it."

As soon as they were home, and Heidi had come out of her sack covering, she started telling grandfather about Peter's cottage.

"Peter's grandmother lies awake at night, afraid that it's going to fall down on them. Tomorrow we must go and help her. We will, won't we, grandfather?" and Heidi looked at grandfather, hopefully.

Grandfather looked at her for some time without speaking. Then he said, "Yes, Heidi, we'll go tomorrow."

The next morning, they went down to Peter's cottage.

As soon as Heidi opened the door and came into the room, grandmother called out from her corner, "It's the child again!" and she stretched out both her hands in welcome.

While Heidi talked to Peter's grandmother, grandfather mended the windows and the roof. Hearing the sound of heavy blows against the wall of the hut, grandmother cried out in alarm, "Ah, my God, the house is going to fall upon us!"

"No, no, grandmother, do not be frightened," Heidi assured her, "it is only grandfather with his hammer. He is mending up everything."

"Is it possible? Is it really possible! So the dear God has not forgotten us!" exclaimed the grandmother.

Brigitta went out to thank Alm Uncle.

However, he gruffly asked her to leave.

"That's enough," he said. "I know what you really think about me."

Then, when it was evening, he carried Heidi back home.

And so the winter went by. After many years of joyless life, Peter's blind grandmother had at last found something to make her happy. Heidi came down to see her whenever it was possible. She would sit by her and tell her everything she knew.

Grandfather often brought hammer and nails with him and mended the cottage. The cottage no longer groaned and rattled and Peter's grandmother was able to sleep in peace. Grandmother said she would never forget what Alm Uncle had done for her.

CHAPTER 5

The Two Visitors

A year passed quickly, and soon, another. Heidi was now eight years old. She had learnt all kinds of useful things from her grandfather and knew how to look after the goats as well as anyone. Little Swan and Little Bear followed her everywhere and gave a bleat of pleasure whenever they heard her voice.

One March morning, when the snow had

melted and Heidi was running around outside, an old gentleman dressed in black arrived at the hut.

"You must be Heidi," he said. "Where is your grandfather?"

He was the old village pastor from Dorfli. He had once been grandfather's neighbor.

"Grandfather's inside, making spoons," said Heidi, looking at the pastor with startled eyes.

The pastor went inside the hut.

"Good morning," he said to grandfather. "It's a long time since I've seen you, neighbor."

Grandfather looked surprised, but pushed a chair towards his guest.

"Sit down," he said.

"I expect you know why I'm here," said the pastor. He nodded towards the window where they could see Heidi outside. "The child should have been at school a year ago."

"I'm not sending her to school," said grandfather. "I'm going to let her grow up and be happy among the goats and birds. She's safe with them and will learn nothing evil."

"But the child is not a goat or a bird! If she does not learn anything evil from them, she would, at the same time, learn nothing at all! This is the last winter she must be allowed to run wild. Next winter she must come to school!"

"No!" replied grandfather. "I cannot send her down the mountain on ice-cold mornings, nor let her return at night when the wind is strong."

"You are right," said the pastor. "And so you must come and live in the village. What sort of life is this? If something happens to you, who would be there to help?"

"I know you mean well," said grandfather, "but I'll not send the child to school. Nor will I come and live in the village."

"Then God help you," said the pastor. And he turned sadly away and went down the mountain.

Grandfather was silent for the rest of that

day and the following morning.

In the evening, soon after dinner, another visitor arrived.

It was Dete. She wore a fine feathered hat and long trailing skirt.

Grandfather studied her from head to foot without saying a word.

"I've come to take Heidi," she told grandfather. "Some rich friends of the lady I work for have a daughter who has to go about in a wheelchair. Her father wants a companion for her - a simple and unspoiled child, not like city children. I thought at once of Heidi. It's a wonderful opportunity. . ."

"Have you nearly finished?" interrupted grandfather, "Because I don't want to hear anything more about it."

Dete became angry.

"What? The child is eight years old and knows nothing! She's my sister's child and I'm responsible for her. I'm not going to give in.

Moreover, I have everybody in Dorfli on my side. And don't even think of fighting this out in court. There are many unpleasant things that could be brought up against you."

"Silence!" thundered the old man. "Go! And never let me see you or your feathered hats again!"

And with that he marched furiously out of the hut.

"You've made grandfather angry," said Heidi, scowling at Dete.

"He'll soon get over it," said Dete. "Show me where your clothes are."

"I'm not coming," answered Heidi.

"Nonsense," continued Dete, "you will have all sorts of good things there."

Then she went to the cupboard, took out Heidi's things, and rolled them up in a bundle.

"I'm not coming," repeated Heidi.

"Don't be so stupid and stubborn," cried Dete. "It's nice in Frankfurt, and if you don't like it, you can come back."

"Can I come back this evening?" said Heidi.

"I've told you that you can come back when you like," said Dete, and hurried the child out of the hut and down the mountain before grandfather came back.

They met Peter outside his cottage.

"Where are you going Heidi?" he called.

"To Frankfurt, for a little visit," said Heidi.

She turned to Dete. "I must say goodbye to grandmother."

"There's no time for that," said Dete, pulling her past the cottage.

Peter ran into the cottage and banged against the table with his bundle of sticks so violently, that everything in the room shook. Grandmother and Peter's mother were alarmed.

"What is the matter, Peter," cried the frightened old woman.

"She is taking Heidi away," explained Peter.

"Who, Peter, where to?" asked the grandmother. But even as she spoke she guessed what had happened, for Brigitta had told her shortly before that she had seen Dete going up to Alm Uncle. She opened the window with trembling hands, and shouted, "Dete! Dete! Please don't take the child away from us!"

But although Dete heard her, she didn't stop.

From that day onwards, Alm Uncle looked fiercer and more forbidding than ever when he came down and passed through Dorfli. All agreed that it was a great mercy the child had got away from him. Only the blind grandmother would have nothing to say against him, and told those who came to her to bring her work how kind and thoughtful he had been with the child, and how many afternoons he had spent mending their house. But most of the people who heard it said that grandmother was too old to understand.

Alm Uncle stopped going to the grand-mother's house. The days were sad again now for the old blind woman, and every day she would murmur, "Dear God, may I see Heidi once more before I die!"

CHAPTER 6

New Place, New People

In her home in Frankfurt, Clara, the little daughter of Herr Sesemann, was lying on the invalid couch in the study, on which she spent the whole day being wheeled from room to room. Her face was thin and pale.

"Isn't it time yet, Fraulein Rottenmeier?" she asked, looking at the clock.

Fraulein Rottenmeier sat at her work-table,

busy with her embroidery. She was the housekeeper and was in charge of the servants whenever Herr Sesemann was away. But before she could reply, a coach arrived at the front door and Dete and Heidi stepped out. A few minutes later, Sebastian, one of the man-servants, brought them into the study.

Fraulein Rottenmeier rose slowly and walked over to see what the little companion for Clara was like. She did not seem very pleased with the child's appearance. Heidi was dressed in her plain little woolen frock, and her old straw hat was bent out of shape.

"What is your name, child?" she asked Heidi.

"Heidi," the answer came.

"That's no name for a child!" said Fraulein Rottenmeier. "What name were you given?"

"I don't remember," replied Heidi.

"What a way to answer!" cried Fraulin Rottenmeier, shaking her head.

"She is in a gentleman's house for the first

time, and does not yet know good manners," Dete said quickly, giving a silent poke to Heidi for giving such an unsuitable answer. "Her name is Adelaide."

"And what age is she?" inquired Fraulein Rottenmeier.

"I do not really remember her exact age," began Dete, "I think she is around ten years old."

"Grandfather told me I was eight," put in Heidi. And Dete gave her another poke.

"What, only eight!" Fraulein Rottenmeier cried angrily. "I didn't expect to see so young a child. Clara is twelve and I wanted a companion of similar age to share her lessons."

"What books do you have for your lessons?" she asked, turning to Heidi.

"None," said Heidi. "I can't read."

"Can't read!" exclaimed Fraulein Rottenmeier. She turned to Dete, but Dete ran from the room with a quick bow.

For a moment, Fraulein Rottenmeier was too amazed to move, but then she hurried after Dete, leaving Heidi in the room. Meanwhile Clara, who had been watching and listening, now beckoned to Heidi.

"Would you rather be called Adelaide or Heidi?" she asked.

"I'm never called anything but Heidi," said Heidi.

"Then that's what I'll call you," said Clara. "Are you happy to come to Frankfurt?"

"No," said Heidi. "But I'll go home again tomorrow and take grandmother a white loaf."

"You are a funny child!" laughed Clara.

Soon, it was time for dinner and Sebastian came to push Clara's chair into the dining room. Heidi went with them. She sat down at the table and found a nice white roll beside her plate.

"Can I have this?" she whispered to Sebastian, who nodded.

Heidi immediately seized the roll and put it into her pocket. Fraulein Rottenmeier had not noticed. She began to tell Heidi all the things she must do and how she must behave if she was going to stay with them. But it had been a long day for Heidi and the little girl was soon fast asleep. Unaware of this, Fraulein Rottenmeier continued with her sermonizing, "Now remember what I said, Adelaide! Have you understood it all?"

"Heidi has been asleep ever so long," said Clara, her face rippling with amusement, for she had not had such an entertaining dinner for a long time.

CHAPTER 7

Kittens for Clara

When Heidi opened her eyes on her first morning in Frankfurt, she could not think where she was. She was in a high, white bed in a very large room. There was a wash-stand in the corner, and near the window were two large chairs and a sofa, both with flower-patterned covers. Heidi jumped out of bed and ran to the windows. She wanted to see the sky and the country, but the window would not open no matter how hard she tried. Then the maid Tinette came and announced that breakfast was ready. But as Heidi had no idea what she was supposed to do now, she sat on a stool and waited for what would happen next.

A little later, Fraulein Rottenmeier appeared and called to Heidi, "What is the matter with you, Adelaide? Don't you understand what breakfast is? Come along at once!"

Clara was already at breakfast by the time Heidi came down. After the meal, Heidi followed Sebastian as he wheeled Clara to the study. As soon as the two children were alone, Heidi asked Clara, "How can one see out from here and look right down on to the ground?"

"You must open the window and look out," replied Clara, amused.

"But the windows won't open," responded Heidi, sadly.

"Sebastian will open one for you," Clara told her.

It was a great relief to Heidi to know that the windows could be opened and she could look out. She was feeling as if she was shut up in prison. Clara now began to ask Heidi questions about her home. Heidi was delighted to tell her all about the mountain and the goats, and the flowery meadows which were so dear to her.

In the afternoon, Heidi told Sebastian that she wanted to ask him something.

"What is it that Miss wants?" asked Sebastian.

"My name is not Miss, it is Heidi."

"Quite so, but I am to call you Miss," explained Sebastian.

Heidi sighed, "Now I have three names!"

"What was it little Miss wished to ask?" said Sebastian.

"How can a window be opened?" asked Heidi.

"Why, like that!" and Sebastian flung up one

of the large windows. Then he brought Heidi a high stool to stand on.

Heidi climbed up, but then drew back her head with a look of great disappointment on her face.

"There is nothing outside but the stony streets," she said. "Where can I go to see over the whole valley?"

"You'd have to climb to the top of that church tower," Sebastian said, pointing out of the window at a church.

A few moments later, Heidi went out of the door and into the street. But the tower was not as near as it had seemed from the window. She went down the street and round several corners, but she was still no closer to it. There were people passing by, but they all seemed in such a hurry that Heidi did not like to ask them the way. Then she came to a corner where a boy was standing carrying a hand-organ and a tortoise.

"How can I get to the church with the tall tower?" she asked him.

"What will you give me if I take you?" he said.

"What would you like to have?" asked Heidi.

"Money?"

"I haven't got any," said Heidi, "but Clara has, and I'm sure she'll give you some."

The boy took her through the streets to the church. Heidi promised the boy more money to wait and show her the way back. Then she pulled the bell rope. An old man opened the church door.

"What do you want?" said the old man, crossly.

"I want to go up the tower," said Heidi. "Please!"

The old man saw how anxious she was.

"All right, I'll take you," he said.

The boy sat down to wait outside and Heidi took the old man's hand as he led her up to the tower. It was a long climb. When they reached the top, the man lifted Heidi up so that she could look out of the open window.

Heidi saw beneath her a sea of roofs, towers and chimney pots.

"It's not at all what I thought," said Heidi in a sad and disappointed voice.

They began to go back down again and passed the tower-keeper's room. Outside the room sat a large, grey cat before a basket of seven kittens.

Heidi peeped inside the basket.

"Oh, the sweet little things!" she cried.

"Would you like to have them?" said the man.

Heidi was overjoyed. There would be plenty of room for them in the large house and what a lovely surprise it would be for Clara.

"But how can I carry them?" asked Heidi.

"I'll bring them to you," he said. "Where do you live?"

"Herr Sesemann's house," said Heidi.

"I know it," said the man. "I'll bring them later."

"May I take two now? One for me and one for Clara?" requested Heidi.

So the man gave her two kittens, one white and the other striped yellow and white. Heidi put one in her left pocket and one in her right. The boy took Heidi back to the house and Sebastian opened the door.

"Hurry, Miss!" said Sebastian, pulling Heidi inside and slamming the door in the boy's face. "Fraulein Rottenmeier has been looking for you. She is furious!"

Heidi walked into the dining room.

Fraulein Rottenmeier who was sitting with a serious face, said, "Adelaide, you have behaved in a very bad way by running out of the house without asking any permission..."

"Meow!" came the answer.

This was enough to make Fraulein

Rottenmeier fly into a temper: "Adelaide! You dare to answer me as if it were a joke?"

"I did not -" began Heidi -"Meow! Meow!"

Fraulein Rottenmeier couldn't take it any more.

"Get up and leave the room!" she commanded.

"It isn't I, it is the kittens!" Heidi blurted out.

"How! What! Kittens!" screamed Fraulein Rottenmeier. "Sebastian! Tinette! Find the horrid things and take them away!" and then she ran into the study and locked the door.

Sebastian, meanwhile, had been trying hard to control his laughter. While serving Heidi, he had seen a kitten's head peeping out of her pocket, and had quite guessed the scene that was to about to take place.

However, now all was quiet and peaceful in the dining room. Clara had the kittens on her lap and Heidi was kneeling next to her. Both were laughing and playing with the tiny animals.

"Sebastian" said Clara, "You must find a bed for the kittens where Fraulein Rottenmeier cannot find them!"

Sebastian promised her that he would do so and made a nice bed for the kittens in a big basket.

Early next morning, the front door bell began to ring loudly. Sebastian opened the door and saw a ragged little boy standing with a hand organ on his back.

"What do you want?" asked Sebastian.

"I want to see Clara!" the boy said. "I want my money!"

"Who told you to come here?" said Sebastian.

"She did," said the boy, pointing at Heidi.

Eventually all was explained. Clara agreed to give the boy the money, but before that she wanted to hear some music from his hand-organ.

The boy started playing at once.

At the same moment, Fraulein Rottenmeier came to see what the noise was about. She was shocked to find a ragged young boy standing in the study, playing his hand-organ in the most energetic way. Clara and Heidi were listening to the music with delight.

"Leave off! Leave off at once!" screamed Fraulein Rottenmeier.

She was rushing angrily towards the boy, when she saw something on the ground crawling towards her feet. It was something dark and dreadful - a tortoise!

Fraulein Rottenmeier jumped up in fear, shrieking with all her might, "Sebastian! Sebastian!"

At once, the organ-player stopped playing. Meanwhile, Sebastian was standing and laughing outside, for he had been peeping to see what was going on. As soon as he entered the room, Fraulein Rottenmeier screamed, "Take them all out! Get the boy and animal away at once!"

Sebastian pulled the boy away, who had by that time quickly picked up the tortoise. When they were outside Sebastian put something into his hand. "This is the four pence from Miss Clara, and another four pence for the music."

The boy went away, happy and satisfied.

Soon after, there was another knock at the door. The old man from the church had arrived with the basket of kittens. They were for Miss Clara, he announced.

"For me?" said Clara, delighted, "Oh, how pretty they are!"

The kittens jumped out of the basket and began running all around the sitting room and even climbed up Fraulein Rottenmeier's dress. Fraulein Rottenmeier was horrified, and climbed up on a chair, calling out loudly, "Tinette! Sebastian! Sebastian!"

Sebastian quickly gathered up the animals and put them back in their basket.

Later, Fraulein Rottenmeier questioned the

servants and discovered that it was Heidi who had caused all the trouble. Growing furious, she called Heidi and told her that she deserved to be punished. She threatened to put Heidi in a dark cellar along with the rats and beetles.

However, Clara intervened. She said that Fraulein Rottenmeier should wait till her father came home. "I will tell him everything, and then he will decide what is to be done with Heidi."

"As you say Clara," said Fraulein Rottenmeier with displeasure. "However, I too shall have something to say to Herr Sesemann."

CHAPTER 8

Meeting Herr Sesemann

Clara grew more and more cheerful day by day and no longer found the lesson hours dull. Heidi continuously jumbled up all the letters and created all sorts of diversions during the lessons. However, the child was still unable to learn to read. And whenever the tutor showed her pictures of birds or animals to help her learn the alphabets, it reminded her of her life on the mountains. "This is a goat! That is a hunter bird!" she would exclaim in a joyful voice.

During the afternoons Heidi would sit with Clara and describe to her the beautiful mountains and her life out there. And while doing so, the longing to return to the mountains would become so overpowering that Heidi always finished with the words, "Now I must go home! Tomorrow I must really go!"

Each time, Clara would try to calm her, and ask her to wait till her father returned. Then they would see what was to be done.

One of the reasons why Heidi agreed to wait was because she had a secret delight. Every day, she could add two more white rolls to the ones she was saving for grandmother. During dinner and supper, Heidi always pocketed the roll placed beside her plate.

Each day, after dinner, Heidi had to sit alone in her room for a few hours. As she had nobody to talk to, she had plenty of time to sit and imagine how everything at home was now turning green, and how the yellow flowers were shining in the sun.

Gradually, Heidi became so homesick, that one day she gathered up all her white rolls and tied them up in her red shawl. Then, she put on her straw hat and went downstairs. After all, Dete had told her she could go home whenever she liked.

But just as she reached the hall-door, she met Fraulein Rottenmeier who was returning from a walk. When she saw Heidi going down the steps outside the house, she at once cried out, "Where are you going? Haven't I told you not to go out in the streets?"

"I'm going home," said Heidi, frightened by the fierce woman.

"You want to go home!" exclaimed Fraulein Rottenmeier. "I should like to know what is wrong with this house! Have you ever had such a house to live in, and such fine food? And have

you ever been so comfortable in your life?"

"No," replied Heidi.

"You ungrateful little thing!" continued the lady, "You get everything you want here. And still you think of nothing but mischief!"

Now Heidi couldn't bear it any more. She poured out all her sorrow.

"But I really, really want to go home! Grandmother is waiting for me; Snowflake would be crying without me; and I can't see the sun say goodnight to the mountains here!"

"Oh my goodness!" cried Fraulein Rottenmeier, her eyes wide with fear. "The child has lost her mind! Sebastian, bring her back in at once."

And she went quickly up the steps.

Sebastian did as he was told. But when he looked more closely at Heidi, he saw that poor child was standing with burning eyes and trembling all over. Sebastian felt sad to see Heidi like this. He put his hand kindly on her shoulder, and took her back to her room, trying to comfort her.

"Don't let her make you unhappy," he said. "Keep your spirits up! We'll go and see the kittens later, shall we?"

That evening, during supper, Heidi sat without moving or eating. All that she did was to quickly hide her roll in her pocket.

Then a day or two later, Fraulein Rottenmeier discovered the heap of white rolls in Heidi's wardrobe.

"What are these!" she cried.

"They're for Peter's grandmother," said Heidi. "Please leave them!"

But Fraulin Rottenmeier ordered Tinette to take the white rolls and Heidi's old straw hat out of her cupboard.

"No! No!" screamed Heidi. "I must keep the hat, and the rolls are for grandmother!"

But Fraulein Rottenmeier ordered Sebastian to throw the rolls away. Poor Heidi ran down to

Clara. "Now grandmother's bread is all gone!" she sobbed.

Clara was upset to see Heidi crying like that.

"Don't cry," she said. "You can have as many rolls as you want when you go home. I promise."

And, at last, Heidi did stop crying.

At supper, Heidi appeared with her eyes red with crying. Sebastian made all sorts of strange signs to her, pointing to his own head and then to hers.

When Heidi got into bed that night she found her old straw hat lying under the coverlet. Sebastian had saved the straw hat for her!

Heidi snatched it up with delight and hugged it joyfully.

A few days after this, Herr Sesemann returned home from Paris. It was late afternoon and he hurried in to see his daughter before doing anything else. Heidi was sitting beside Clara.

Father and daughter greeted each other warmly.

Then Herr Sesemann said, "So, this is our little Swiss girl."

"Yes, this is Heidi," said Clara.

Fraulein Rottenmeier was waiting for him in the dining room and quickly told him how unhappy she was about Heidi. "If you only knew the things she did and the animals she brought into the house! Her behavior is most peculiar and shocking. At times, it seems as if she's not in her right mind."

After dinner, Herr Sesemann went to the study and sat down beside his daughter.

"Little one, will you fetch me a glass of fresh water?" he asked Heidi.

Heidi disappeared at once.

"Tell me about Heidi," Herr Sesemann said to Clara, "and about the animals, and why Fraulein Rottenmeier thinks Heidi's not in the right mind sometimes."

Clara laughed and she told him about the

kittens and about the boy with the hand-organ.

Her father laughed with her on hearing all this. "So you don't want me to send the child home again?" he asked.

"Oh no," said Clara. "It used to be so dull, but something fresh happens every day now and she tells me stories about the mountain."

At that moment Heidi came with a glass of water.

"Have you brought me some nice fresh water?" Herr Sesemann asked as Heidi handed him the glass.

"Yes, fresh from the pump," answered Heidi.

"You did not go yourself to the pump?" asked Clara.

"Yes, I did; it is quite fresh. I had to go a long way, and a gentleman with the white hair asked me to give his kind regards to Herr Sesemann."

"You have had quite a successful expedition," said Herr Sesemann laughing, "and who was the gentleman?"

"He was kind and laughed, and he had a thick gold chain and a horse's head at the top of his stick," described Heidi.

"It's the doctor," exclaimed Clara and her father at the same moment.

That evening, Herr Sesemann informed Fraulein Rottenmeier that Heidi was to stay.

"The child must be treated kindly," he said.

He also told her that his mother was shortly expected in the house on a long visit.

Herr Sesemann went back to Paris after two weeks. The day before Frau Sesemann, Herr Sesemann's mother was expected, Fraulein Rottenmeier warned Heidi not to call Frau Sesemann 'grandmamma', but always as 'madam'.

Poor Heidi was puzzled to hear this.

CHAPTER 9

Another Grandmother

The following evening, preparations for Frau Sesemann's arrival were in full swing. Tinette had a new white cap on her head, and Fraulein Rottenmeier went about surveying everything. Soon, Clara's grandmother arrived and straight away went to see her granddaughter. A little later, Tinette told Heidi to go downstairs into the study.

Heidi opened the study door and walked right up to Clara's grandmother.

"Good-evening, Mrs. Madam," she said.

"Well!" said the grandmother, laughing, "is that how they address people in your home on the mountain?"

"No," replied Heidi, gravely, "I never knew any one with that name before."

"Nor I either," said Clara's grandmother, patting Heidi's cheek, "When I am with children, I am always called 'grandmamma'."

Grandmamma attracted Heidi. She had beautiful white hair, and two long lace ends hung down from the cap on her head. Each time the grandmother moved, the lace waved gently about her face as if a soft breeze was blowing around her.

"What is your name, child?" grandmamma asked her.

"I am always called Heidi; but now I am to be called Adelaide!" said Heidi.

Fraulein Rottenmeier interrupted Heidi, "Frau Sesemann will surely agree with me that it was necessary to choose a name that could be pronounced easily."

"My dear Rottenmeier," replied grandmamma, "if a person is called 'Heidi', I call her by that name."

Clara's grandmother was an alert old lady. She knew what was going on in the house as soon as she entered it.

The next afternoon, when Clara was asleep on the couch as usual, grandmamma asked Fraulein Rottenmeier to bring Heidi to her room.

"She's bored and lonely," she told the housekeeper. "I've some books I'd like to give her. "She can't read," said Fraulein Rottenmeier. "The tutor has tried to teach her, but without success."

"That's strange," said the old lady. "Well, bring her to me. She can look at the pictures."

Heidi came and gazed with delight and wonder at the beautiful colored pictures in the books. All of a sudden, as she looked at a page, Heidi started sobbing.

Grandmamma looked at the picture – it showed a green pasture full of young animals, grazing and others nibbling at the shrubs. In the middle was a shepherd leaning upon his staff and looking on at his happy flock.

Grandmamma put a hand on Heidi's shoulder.

"Don't cry," she said in a kindly voice. "I think the picture has reminded you of something. But there's a beautiful story to the picture which I shall tell you this evening."

After a while, seeing that Heidi had calmed down a bit she asked, "Now, I want you to tell me something. How are you getting on with your lessons? Have you learned a lot?"

"Oh no," replied Heidi. "But I knew I wouldn't learn to read. It is too difficult."

"And who told you that?" asked grandmamma.

"Peter told me, for he tried and tried and could not learn."

"Peter must be a very odd boy then! But Heidi, you must not always go by what Peter says. You must try for yourself. Now you'll try and you'll soon learn to read. And when you do, you can have that book for your own."

Heidi had listened attentively to grand-mamma's words. Now she exclaimed with a big sigh, "Oh! If only I could read now!"

Since the day Heidi had so much wanted to return home, and Fraulein Rottenmeier had scolded her and told her how ungrateful and wicked her behavior was, a change had come over the child. She now understood that she could not go home whenever she wished as Dete had told her, but that she would have to stay in Frankfurt for a long, long time; perhaps for ever! She also understood that if she wished to leave, Herr Sesemann, and even Clara and

grandmamma would think her ungrateful. So, there was nobody whom Heidi could tell of her misery. But her little heart grew heavy with sadness. Often at night, she lay awake for long hours thinking of grandfather and the mountain. Often, she would cry quietly into her pillow, so that no one might hear her.

However, Heidi's unhappiness did not escape grandmamma's eyes. She observed that the child ate very little and was becoming thin and pale.

"What's the matter, Heidi?" she asked one day.

"Oh no!" cried Heidi. "I can't tell anyone."

"Then this is what you must do," said grandmamma. "Whenever we're in great trouble and can't speak to anyone about it, we must pray to God for help."

"But I never say any prayers," said Heidi.

"That is the reason you are so unhappy," said grandmamma, "because you know no one who can help you. Tell everything to God, and pray to Him. He can give the help that no one else can give."

"Can I tell Him everything?" said Heidi.

"Everything," grandmamma told her.

So Heidi ran to her room, put her hands together and told God about everything that was making her sad. She begged Him to let her go home to grandfather and the mountain.

About a week after this, the tutor came to see Frau Sesemann.

"A most surprising thing has happened," he told her. "Heidi has learned to read practically overnight!"

"Many unlikely things happen in this life," said Frau Sesemann, with a twinkle in her eye. After the tutor had gone, Frau Sesemann went downstairs and found Heidi sitting beside Clara, reading aloud to her.

That evening, Heidi found the large book with the beautiful pictures lying beside her place at dinner. She looked up at grandmamma.

"Is it really mine now?" she asked.

Frau Sesemann smiled. "Yes, it is yours now."

"Mine, to keep always?" said Heidi, blushing with pleasure, "Even when I go home?"

"Yes, yours for ever," grandmamma assured her. "Tomorrow we'll begin to read it."

From that day onwards Heidi's chief pleasure was to read the stories which belonged to the beautiful pictures, over and over again.

The days passed by quickly enough and soon it was time for grandmamma to return home.

One day, in the last week of her visit, grandmamma called Heidi to her room and asked, "Are you still troubled, Heidi?"

Heidi nodded in reply.

"Have you told God about it?"

"Yes," said Heidi.

"And do you pray to Him every day?"

"No, I have left off praying."

"Do not tell me that, Heidi!" exclaimed grandmamma. "Why have you left off praying?"

"It's of no use, God doesn't listen. I've prayed every day for weeks, but God hasn't done what I asked."

"God knows better than we do what is good for us," said grandmamma. "If we ask Him for something that isn't good for us, He doesn't give it; but He gives something better! You must go on praying and trusting in Him."

Grandmamma's words went straight to Heidi's heart.

"I'll ask God to forgive me," said she, "and I'll never forget Him again."

The house seemed silent and empty after grandmamma went away. Clara and Heidi sat during the rest of the day like two lost children. The next day, as Heidi was reading a story about a dying grandmother, she cried, "Oh Clara, Peter's grandmother is dead!" and she burst into tears. For everything Heidi read was so real to her, that she thought it was the grandmother at home who had died.

Clara tried hard to explain to Heidi that the story in the book was about quite a different grandmother. When Heidi was finally convinced, a new thought occurred to her and she began to weep again. She thought that perhaps the grandmother, and even the grandfather might die while she was so far way. And that, if she did not go home for a long time, she would never be able to see them any more!

At this moment, Fraulein Rottenmeier came into the room and Clara explained what had happened. Fraulein Rottenmeier grew quite irritated to hear this.

"That's enough now! Stop crying," she told Heidi. "If there are any more scenes like this, I'll take the book away from you."

At these words, Heidi turned white with fear. The book was her one great treasure. She quickly dried her tears and never cried again while reading.

But she lost her appetite and became pale and thin. At night, she would remember her home and weep, burying her head into the pillow so that her crying might not be heard by anybody.

CHAPTER 10

A Ghost in the House

For the past few days, something very strange and mysterious was happening in Herr Sesemann's house. Every morning, when Sebastian or John (another of the servants) went downstairs, they found the front door wide open for no apparent reason. At first, they thought a thief had got in, but nothing was missing from the house. Finally, Fraulein

Rottenmeier persuaded Sebastian and John to sit up and watch at night.

The two sat up to watch as decided. However, soon they became sleepy and began to drowse. When midnight struck, Sebastian woke up. Everything was dead silent. Sebastian started feeling frightened and called out to his companion. John, however, was fast asleep. Then, after a lot of shaking, he finally got up at about one o' clock. Then, remembering why he was sitting in a chair instead of lying in his bed, he said, "Come, Sebastian, we must go outside and see what is going on."

Then he opened the door and went into the hall. But as soon as he did so, a gust of wind blew out the light in his hand. John started back, almost overthrowing Sebastian, and quickly shut the door. He was trembling all over and was as white as a ghost.

"What's the matter?" asked Sebastian. "What did you see?"

"I saw the door partly open," gasped John, "and a white figure standing at the top of the steps."

Sebastian felt his blood run cold. The two sat down close to one another and did not move again until it was morning and the streets were bustling with people and traffic.

When Fraulein Rottenmeier heard about this, she immediately wrote to Herr Sesemann, telling him that he must come home owing to the ghostly happenings in his house.

At first, Herr Sesemann did not pay much heed to this ghost tale, and replied that he was quite busy and would not be able to come.

Then, Fraulein Rottenmeier went to the children and in a low mysterious voice told Clara and Heidi about the ghost in the house. At once, Clara grew extremely excited and declared that her father must come home at once. So, Fraulein Rottenmeier again wrote to Herr Sesemann informing him that the events were having an adverse effect on Clara's health. Herr Sesemann, concerned for his daughter, immediately returned to Frankfurt.

Once he had been to Clara's room and had satisfied himself that she was well, his anxiety died down. Then, he called Sebastian to him.

"Have you or any of the other servants been playing tricks, Sebastian?" he asked.

"No Sir!" said Sebastian, "On my honor!"

"Then you should be ashamed of yourself, Sebastian, a great strong lad like you, to run away from a ghost! Now go and take a message to my old friend the doctor. Give him my kind regards and ask him to come tonight at nine o'clock."

The doctor was a silver-haired man with kindly eyes and an anxious expression on his face. "Is someone ill?" he asked, when he arrived that evening.

"Much worse than that, doctor," said Herr Sesemann. "There's a ghost in the house. My house is haunted."

The doctor started laughing loudly on hearing this. But Herr Sesemann told him how the front door of the house was mysteriously opened each night by somebody. And so, he had decided to keep watch along with the doctor to find out who the culprit was.

The two men armed themselves with loaded revolvers and waited in the same room where Sebastian and John had kept watch. Two good sized lamps had also been lit, for Herr Sesemann was determined not to wait for any ghosts in half-darkness.

One o'clock struck and everything was quiet. Suddenly, the doctor lifted a finger. "Sesemann, do you hear something?" he whispered.

They both listened - and heard a key being turned and a door being opened.

Herr Sesemann picked up his revolver as well as one of the lights. The doctor did the

same and the two men crept into the hall.

Moonlight streamed through the open front door and fell on a white figure standing motionless in the doorway.

"Who's there?" thundered the doctor.

The figure turned and gave a low cry.

There, in her little white nightgown, stood Heidi. She was staring wild-eyed at the lights and revolvers and trembling all over.

"It's your little Swiss girl, Sesemann!" said the doctor.

"Child, what does this mean?" said Herr Sesemann, "Why did you come down here?"

Heidi was white with terror. She answered, "I don't know."

But now the doctor stepped forward.

"This is a matter for me, Sesemann," he said. "I must take the child upstairs to her bed."

The doctor gently took Heidi's hand and led her up to her bedroom.

"Don't be frightened," he said as they went

up side by side, "it's quite all right."

Then he carefully laid the child on her bed and sat down beside her.

Gradually, Heidi became calmer and stopped trembling. The doctor held her hand.

"Now tell me where you wanted to go?" he said. "Had you been dreaming?"

"Yes," said Heidi. "I dream the same dream every night. I think I'm back with grandfather and I hear the sound of the fir trees outside and I see the stars shining. Then I open the door quickly and run out and it's all so beautiful. But when I wake up, I'm still in Frankfurt."

"Are you happy here in Frankfurt?" asked the doctor.

"Yes," came the quiet reply, but it sounded more like "No."

"And where did you live with your grandfather?"

"Up on the mountain," answered Heidi.

"Wasn't that rather dull at times?" said the doctor.

"No, no, it was beautiful, beautiful!" said Heidi and she began to cry as she remembered all the things she was missing.

The doctor stood up, "There, there, crying will do you good, and then go to sleep. Tomorrow everything will be all right."

Then, he went downstairs to speak with Herr Sesemann.

"The child is walking in her sleep because she's unhappy," he said. "She's so homesick and ill. You must send her home, Sesemann, tomorrow!"

Herr Sesemann was pacing up and down the room in the greatest state of anxiety.

"What!" he exclaimed, "The child a sleep-walker and ill! All this has taken place in my house and no one has known anything about it! And I am to send back the child who came here happy and healthy, miserable and ill?

I can't do such a thing! Cure the child doctor, and then she shall go home; but you must do something first."

"Sesemann," replied the doctor, "Heidi's illness cannot be cured with pills and powders. If you send her back at once she may recover in the mountain air, if not... You would rather she went back ill than not at all?"

Herr Sesemann stood still; the doctor's words were a shock to him.

CHAPTER 11

On the Mountain Again

Herr Sesemann quickly went upstairs and knocked loudly at Fraulein Rottenmeier's door. The lady awoke from sleep with a cry of alarm. She heard Herr Sesemann calling to her from the other side of the door, "Please come down to me in the dining-room; we must prepare for a journey at once."

Fraulein Rottenmeier looked at her clock: it

was just half-past four; she had never got up so early before in her life. What could have happened? Herr Sesemann instructed her to get out a trunk at once and pack up all the things belonging to Heidi, and a good part of Clara's dresses as well, so that the child might take home proper clothing. But everything was to be done immediately.

While Fraulein Rottenmeier stared in astonishment at Herr Sesemann's sudden instructions, he went to speak to Clara. Clara was upset when her father told her that Heidi was going home. She made all sorts of suggestions for keeping Heidi with her, but her father was firm. He promised to take her to Switzerland the next summer if she made no further fuss. So Clara gave in, but asked if she could put some things in a box for Heidi. Her father gladly agreed to this suggestion.

Then Herr Sesemann went off to his study and wrote a letter for Heidi's grandfather.

Then he sent for Sebastian and told him that he was to travel with Heidi, giving him a letter to carry to the grandfather that would explain everything.

Meanwhile, Heidi had been woken up by Tinette, dressed in her Sunday frock and was waiting anxiously to see what would happen next. For Tinette had explained nothing to her.

Herr Sesemann went back to the dining-room. Breakfast was now ready, and he asked for Heidi.

Heidi was brought, and she walked up to him and said, "Good-morning."

Herr Sesemann looked inquiringly into her face and said, "Well, what do you say to this, little one?"

Heidi gave him a puzzled look.

"I see you know nothing about it," he laughed. "You're going home today."

"Home?" murmured Heidi. She turned pale and found it difficult to breathe.

"Don't you want to go?"

"Oh yes, yes!" she cried. By now her face had become rosy with delight.

"All right, then," said Herr Sesemann, "now sit down and have your breakfast."

However, Heidi was too excited to eat her breakfast, and so Herr Sesemann instructed Sebastian to pack some food to take with them.

"Now run upstairs and sit with Clara in her room," he added kindly, turning to Heidi.

Clara showed Heidi the things she had put in a box — dresses, aprons, and handkerchiefs.

"And look here," said Clara, holding up a basket. Heidi peeped in and jumped for joy.

Inside were twelve white rolls for Peter's grandmother!

Then someone called, "The carriage is here!"

Heidi ran to her room to bring her book, straw hat and shawl. Then she said her good-byes to Clara, Herr Sesemann, Fraulein Rottenmeier, and everyone else, and climbed into the carriage with Sebastian.

"Say goodbye and thank you to the doctor for me," she called back as the carriage pulled away.

Heidi was soon sitting in the railway carriage, holding her basket tightly on her lap. For many hours she sat as still as a mouse. It was only now she was beginning to realize that she was going home to grandfather, the mountain, grandmother, and Peter! Pictures of all she was going to see again rose one by one before her eyes. Then, all of a sudden, she said anxiously, "Sebastian, are you sure that grandmother on the mountain is not dead?"

"No, no," said Sebastian, wishing to soothe her, "she is sure to be alive still."

After a while, Heidi fell asleep. She did not wake till Sebastian shook her by the arm and called to her, "Wake up, wake up! We shall have to get out directly; we are just in Basle!"

There was a further railway journey of

many hours the next day. Heidi again sat with her basket on her knee. Her excitement increased with every mile of the journey. All of a sudden, before Heidi expected it, a voice called out, "Mayenfield!"

Heidi and Sebastian both jumped up. In another minute they were both standing on the platform with Heidi's trunk. Outside the station was a man with a horse and cart.

"Which is the safest way to Dorfli?" Sebastian asked him. "And how can a box be taken there?"

"All roads here are safe," was the reply. "I'm going to Dorfli myself. Do you want me to take that box?"

"I can go by myself, I know the way well from Dorfli," put in Heidi.

It was finally agreed that the man should take both Heidi and the box on his cart to Dorfli, which was a great relief to Sebastian.

He gave Heidi the letter for her grandfather

and a parcel which he said was a present from Herr Sesemann. The cart rolled away in the direction of the mountains, while Sebastian, glad of having no tiring and dangerous journey on foot before him, went back to the station platform to await a return train.

The driver of the car was the miller at Dorfli, and was taking home his sacks of flour. He had never seen Heidi, but like everybody in Dorfli knew all about her.

"You are the child who lived with your grandfather, Alm Uncle, are you not?"

"Yes."

"Didn't they treat you well down there that you have come back so soon?"

"It was not that; everything in Frankfurt is as nice as it could be."

"Then why are you running home again?"

"Because I would a thousand times rather be with grandfather on the mountain than anywhere else in the world."

The miller was very surprised to hear this.

The clock was striking five when they reached Dorfli. A crowd of women and children immediately surrounded the cart, for the box and the child arriving with the miller had aroused everybody's curiosity. As the miller put Heidi down, she thanked him saying, "Grandfather will come for the box."

Then she began climbing the steep mountain path as quickly as she could. One thought filled her mind - was Peter's grandmother still alive? Then she caught sight of grandmother's cottage and her heart began to beat faster. She ran to the doorway, unable to make a sound.

"Dear God," a voice came from inside. "That is how Heidi used to run in. Who is there?"

"It's me, grandmother!" cried Heidi, and she ran and threw her arms around the old woman, unable to speak for joy.

The old woman herself could not say a

word for some time, so unexpected was this happiness; but at last she put out her hand and stroked Heidi's curly head. "Yes, yes, that's her hair and her voice," she said, "God has answered my prayers."

And tears of joy fell from the blind eyes on to Heidi's hand. "Is it really you, Heidi; have you really come back to me?"

"Yes, grandmother, I am really here," answered Heidi. "Do not cry, for I have really come back and I am never going away again. I shall come every day to see you, and you won't have any more hard bread to eat for some days, for look, look!"

And Heidi took the rolls from the basket and piled them all in grandmother's lap.

"Ah child, what a blessing you bring with you!" the old woman exclaimed, as she felt the soft rolls. "But you're the greatest blessing of all, Heidi!"

And again she touched Heidi's hair and said,

"Say something so that I may hear your voice. Tell me everything you've been doing."

And Heidi told her how unhappy she had been and how she had been afraid she would never see grandmother and the mountains again.

Peter's mother now came in and stood for a moment overcome with astonishment.

"Why, it's Heidi!" she exclaimed, "Grandmother, if you could only see her, and see what a pretty frock she has on. And the hat with the feather in it is yours too, I suppose?"

"You can have it if you like it," said Heidi.

But Brigitta would not think of taking such a beautiful hat. And so, Heidi hid the hat quietly in a corner behind grandmother's chair. Then she took off her pretty dress and put her red shawl on over her.

"Now I must go home to see grandfather," she said, eventually. "I'll come back again tomorrow. Goodnight, grandmother."

"Why have you taken off that pretty dress?" asked Brigitta.

"Perhaps grandfather might not know me otherwise," replied Heidi.

Heidi continued her way up the mountain, her basket on her arm.

All around were the steep, green slopes, bright in the evening sun. Suddenly, a warm, red glow fell on everything, and the two mountain peaks above seemed like two great flames. As she stood gazing around her at all this splendor, tears of happiness came into Heidi's eyes and she thanked God for being home. Then she ran on quickly, and in a very little while she could see the tops of the fir trees above the hut roof, then the roof itself, and at last the whole hut. And there was grandfather, sitting on the bench seat as always, smoking his pipe.

Quicker and quicker went her little feet, and before Alm Uncle had time to see who was coming, Heidi had rushed up to him, thrown down her basket and flung her arms round his neck, saying, "Grandfather! Grandfather! Grandfather!" over and over again.

The old man could not speak for some minutes. For the first time in many years, his eyes were wet. Then he put Heidi on his knees and said, "So, you've come back to me, Heidi. Did they send you away?"

"Oh no, grandfather," said Heidi, "You mustn't think that. They were all so kind - Clara and her father and Frau Rottenmeier. But all I wanted was to come home to you. Perhaps it's all in the letter…" and Heidi jumped down and fetched the parcel and the letter and handed them both to her grandfather.

There was some money in the parcel. "That belongs to you," said grandfather. Then he read the letter, and without a word put it inside his pocket.

"Do you think you can still drink milk with

me, Heidi?" he asked, taking the child by the hand to go into the hut. Heidi skipped into the hut after her grandfather. She was delighted to see everything again.

"Now come and have your milk," said grandfather. Heidi sat down on her high stool, and drank her milk eagerly.

"Our milk tastes nicer than anything else in the world, grandfather," she exclaimed.

A shrill whistle was heard outside. It was Peter with the goats. Heidi ran out to them. Seeing Heidi, Peter stood still with astonishment, and gazed speechlessly at her.

"Good evening, Peter," she said. "Little Swan! Little Bear! Do you know me again?"

The animals immediately began rubbing their heads against her, bleating with pleasure.

Heidi was filled with delight at being among all her old friends again; she flung her arms round the pretty little Snowflake, while she herself was thrust at from all sides by the affectionate and confiding goats.

At last, she got near to Peter who hadn't yet got over his surprise.

"Come here Peter," cried Heidi, "and say good-evening to me."

"So, you're back," said Peter finally, and took Heidi's hand which she was holding out in greeting, "Will you come out with me tomorrow?"

"Not tomorrow, but perhaps the day after, for tomorrow I must go down to grandmother," replied Heidi.

"I am glad you are back," said Peter, while his whole face beamed with pleasure.

When Heidi went inside, she found her bed already made up for her. The hay was fresh, and grandfather had carefully spread and tucked in the clean sheets.

It was with a happy heart that Heidi lay down on her hay-bed that night, and she slept more soundly than she had for a year.

Grandfather got up at least ten times during the night and climbed up the ladder to see if Heidi was all right. But Heidi did not stir; she had no need now to wander about, for she was at home again on the mountain.

CHAPTER 12

Heidi Narrates a Story

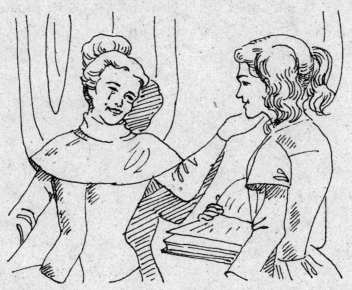

The next day, grandfather came down with Heidi to Peter's cottage. He left her there and went on down to Dorfli to fetch her box. As Heidi ran inside the hut, grandmother heard her approaching steps and greeted her, "Is it you, child? Have you come again?"

Then she told Heidi how much she had enjoyed the first of the white rolls, and already felt stronger and healthier.

Suddenly, a brilliant thought came to Heidi. "Oh, I have lots of money, grandmother," she cried excitedly, skipping about the room in her delight, "and I know now what I will do with it. You must have a fresh white roll every day. Peter can bring them up from Dorfli."

"No, no, child!" answered grandmother, "I cannot let you do that; the money was not given to you for that purpose; you must give it to your grandfather, and he will tell you how you are to spend it."

But Heidi continued to jump about, saying over and over again in a tone of ecstasy, "Now, grandmother can have a roll every day and will grow quite strong again… and, oh, grandmother," she suddenly caught sight of the old song book and had an idea. "I can read now," she cried. "Shall I read you one of the hymns from your book?"

"Oh yes!" said grandmother, surprised and

delighted. "But can you really read, child?"

By then, Heidi had already taken down the book and wiped it carefully. Now she sat down on a stool beside the grandmother and asked her which hymn she should read.

"What you like, child, what you like," said grandmother.

So Heidi read out a song about the sun from the book.

Tears of joy filled grandmother's eyes.

"Ah Heidi," she said. "You have brought me such comfort!"

Soon after, there was a knock at the window, and Heidi saw grandfather beckoning her to come home.

"I have to go now," she told grandmother. "But I'll come again tomorrow."

As she was going out, Brigitta ran to her with the frock and hat she had left. Heidi put the dress over her arm, but asked Brigitta to keep the hat.

Heidi was so full of her morning's doings that she at once began to tell her grandfather about them. "If grandmother won't take the money, grandfather, will you give it all to me, and I can then give Peter enough every day to buy a roll and two on Sunday?" she asked.

"The money is yours, do what you like with it," said grandfather. "You can buy bread for grandmother for many, many years with it."

Heidi was very happy.

"I'm so glad God didn't let me have my way at once," she told her grandfather. "If I'd come home when I first wanted to, I should not have been able to read the hymns to grandmother. God arranges things so much better than us, doesn't he grandfather?"

"Where did you learn about God, Heidi?" asked grandfather.

"From Clara's grandmother," said Heidi. She said that God never forgets us, even if we forget Him."

"But supposing one forgets Him? What happens then?"

"Then everything goes wrong," said Heidi.

"And so no one can ever go back," said grandfather, with a serious look on his face.

"Oh, no, grandfather, we can go back," said Heidi, and she narrated the story about a son who goes away from his father and wastes all his money. But when he returns home, his father doesn't turn him away. Instead, he welcomes him with open arms.

"Isn't the story of the prodigal son a beautiful story, grandfather?"

"Yes, Heidi," grandfather replied softly. "It's a beautiful story."

And after Heidi was asleep that night, grandfather went up the ladder and looked at the sleeping child. Her hands were still folded as if she had fallen asleep saying her prayers. There was an expression of peace and trust on the little face. Grandfather gazed down at her for a

long time. Then, he too folded his hands, bowed his head, and said, "Father, I have sinned before thee and am not worthy to be called thy son."

And two large tears rolled down the old man's cheeks.

The next day was Sunday. Heidi heard the sound of church bells drifting up from the valley. "Put on your best frock, Heidi," said grandfather. "We're going to church together."

He was wearing his best coat and trousers.

"Oh grandfather!" cried Heidi. "You do look nice."

The church service had begun when Heidi and her grandfather went in through the door of the building.

The people were singing a hymn, but soon everyone was nudging each other and whispering, "Did you see? Alm Uncle is in church!"

When the service was over, Alm Uncle took Heidi by the hand, and walked towards the pastor's house. Everyone noticed how friendly he looked, and how kindly he behaved towards the child.

"See, how carefully he took the little one by the hand," said one.

And the miller said, "Did I not tell you so from the first? What child would run away from where she had everything of the best, to a grandfather who was cruel and unkind, and of whom she was afraid?"

And so, everybody began to feel quite friendly towards Alm Uncle.

Meanwhile, grandfather had gone to speak to the pastor.

"You were right and I was wrong," he said. "I'll find a house in Dorfli for the winter months and Heidi shall go to school."

The pastor's kindly eyes shone with pleasure.

"You will not repent coming to live with us again. As for me, you will always be welcome as a dear friend and neighbor," said he, shaking hands with grandfather at the door.

When grandfather came out of the pastor's house, everyone came forward to greet him and shake him by the hand. There was such a general chorus of pleasure that any one would have thought Alm Uncle was the most beloved person in all Dorfli.

At last, as the old man stood alone with the child, there was a radiant light on his face.

"I am happier today than I deserve," he told Heidi, "God was good to me when He sent you to my hut."

When they reached Peter's home, grandfather opened the door and walked straight in. "Good-morning, grandmother," he said.

"Dear God, if it is not Uncle!" cried grandmother in pleased surprise. "That I should live to see such a thing! And now I can thank you for all that you have done for me. May God reward you dear Uncle!"

Grandmother stretched out a trembling hand

to him, and the grandfather shook it warmly.

"And I have a prayer to make to you!" said grandmother. "Please do not send the child away again before I lie under the grass. Oh, you do not know what that child is to me!" and she clasped Heidi to her.

"Don't be afraid, grandmother," said Uncle in a reassuring voice, "I shall not punish either you or myself by doing so. We are all together now, and let's pray to God that we may continue so for long."

At this moment, Peter rushed in, clearly in a great hurry. Gasping and breathless he held out a letter. It was addressed to Heidi and had been delivered at the post office in Dorfli. Heidi opened the letter at once and read it without hesitation.

The letter was from Clara. She wrote that the house had been dull since Heidi left; and she had at last persuaded her father to take her to the baths at Ragatz in the coming autumn.

Grandmamma would join them there, and they both were looking forward to paying Heidi and her grandfather a visit. Grandmamma sent a further message that she was sending some coffee to go with the rolls, for grandmother.

There were exclamations of pleasure on hearing the good news.

CHAPTER 13

Preparations for a Journey

The doctor was walking towards Herr
Sesemann's house one sunny morning in
September. There was an expression of
sadness on his face, and his hair had grown
greyer since the spring. Just a few
months before, his only daughter had died.
He had never been the same bright and cheery
man since.

Sebastian opened the door to him, and greeted him respectfully.

"Everything as usual, Sebastian?" asked the doctor in his pleasant voice as he went up the stairs.

"I am glad you have come, doctor," exclaimed Herr Sesemann, as the latter entered. "We must talk about this Swiss journey; do you still want to cancel the trip, even though Clara is definitely improving in health?"

"My dear Sesemann, I have never seen such a man as you!" said the doctor. "I really wish our mother was here; she would soon put everything right. You sent for me three times yesterday only to ask me the same question!"

"Yes, I know," said Herr Sesemann, "But you must understand, dear friend, I don't have the courage to refuse Clara what I have been promising her all along. For months now she has been living on the thought of

133

meeting Heidi this autumn."

"You must do it, Sesemann," said the doctor. "Clara has never had such a bad summer, and so this tiring journey is out of the question for her. Next May, she shall be taken to the baths and stay there for the cure until the weather is quite hot. Then she can be carried up the mountain from time to time when she is stronger."

Herr Sesemann had listened to the doctor in silence. Now, he suddenly jumped up. "Doctor," he said, "tell me the truth. Do you have any hope of her final recovery?"

"Very little," the doctor replied, quietly. "But, friend, you still have her with you. Think of my lonely house!"

Herr Sesemann was now pacing up and down the room, deeply engaged in thought. Suddenly, he came to a halt beside his friend and laid his hand on his shoulder.

"Doctor, I have an idea," said Herr

Sesemann. "You too are not quite well and need a change. Why don't you go and visit Heidi yourself? The mountain air would do you good, don't you think?"

It was a bitter disappointment to Clara to give up the journey. However, she knew that her father would never refuse her a thing unless he was certain that it would be harmful for her. So, she tried to hide her sadness as well as she could.

"Dear doctor, you will go and see Heidi, won't you?" she pleaded. "And then you can come and tell me all about it. I promise to take as much cod liver oil as you like if you go."

Hearing this, the doctor smiled and said, "Then I must certainly go, Clara, for you will then become strong and healthy. When should I start?"

"Tomorrow morning, early if possible," replied Clara.

The doctor could not help laughing. "Next

you would be scolding me for not being there already! Well, I must go and make arrangements for the journey."

But Clara would not let him go until she had given him endless messages for Heidi. She informed him that she would send the presents later, as Fraulein Rottenmeier must first help her to pack them up. The doctor promised to follow Clara's directions faithfully. While he was going downstairs, he heard Clara instructing Tinette to fill up a box with soft cakes.

The doctor was hurrying away when he met Fraulein Rottenmeier who was returning from her walk. He informed her of his intended journey, and begged her to pack up the parcels for Heidi as she alone knew how to pack.

Fraulein Rottenmeier went quickly inside. She cleared a large table so that all the things for Heidi could be spread out upon it, and packed under Clara's own eyes. It was no light job, for the presents were of all shapes and sizes. There was a little warm cloak with a hood for Heidi, a thick warm shawl and a large box full of cakes for grandmother, an immense sausage for Peter, and a packet of tobacco for grandfather. Finally, there were a lot of mysterious little bags, and parcels, and boxes for Heidi.

CHAPTER 14

The Doctor Arrives

The early light of morning fell upon the mountains, and a fresh breeze rustled through the fir trees. The sound awoke Heidi, and she opened her eyes. Jumping out of her bed, she dressed herself as quickly as she could.

Grandfather had already left the hut and was standing outside.

"Good-morning, grandfather!" cried Heidi, running out.

"What, you are awake already?" he said, giving her a morning greeting.

Then he went inside the shed, milked the goats, brushed and washed them, and brought them out of their shed.

At this moment, Peter's shrill whistle was heard and all the goats came along, leaping and springing.

"Can you come out with me today?" he asked Heidi.

"I am afraid I cannot, Peter," she answered. "I am expecting the visitors from Frankfurt. I must be at home when they come."

"You have said the same thing for days now," grumbled Peter, and then he turned and went off, swinging his stick angrily through the air.

Heidi went inside the hut. Since the time she had come back from Frankfurt, she had kept the hut neat and orderly. Every morning, she went about the room, putting everything in its place. After that, she fetched a duster, climbed on a chair, and rubbed the table till it shone again. When grandfather came in later, he would look around and say to himself, "We look like Sunday every day now; Heidi did not go abroad for nothing."

And so today, after Peter had left, Heidi went about doing her everyday chores. When it was done, she came out and started jumping to the tune of the swinging fir trees.

Suddenly, she called out, "Grandfather! Come, come!"

Grandfather stepped out and saw Heidi running towards where the mountain path descended, crying, "They are coming! They are coming! And the doctor is in front!"

Heidi rushed forward to welcome her old friend, who held out his hands in greeting to her.

"Now take me to your grandfather, Heidi," said the doctor, "and show me where you live."

But Heidi still remained standing, looking down the path with a questioning gaze. "Where are Clara and grandmother?" she asked.

"You see, Heidi, Clara was very ill and could not travel," replied the doctor. "But next spring, when the days grow warm and long again, they will come here."

Heidi stood motionless for a second or two, overcome by the unexpected disappointment. Then she lifted her eyes and saw the sad expression in the doctor's eyes as he looked down at her. She had never seen him so sad when she was in Frankfurt. It went to Heidi's heart; she could not bear to see anybody unhappy, especially her dear doctor. So, she began to think how she might console him.

"Oh, it won't be very long to wait for spring, and then they will be sure to come," she said in a reassuring voice. "Now let us go and find grandfather."

Hand in hand with her friend, she climbed

up to the hut.

Grandfather greeted his guest warmly. Then the two men sat down in front of the hut, and the doctor asked Heidi to sit beside him. Then he whispered to her that something was being brought up the mountain for her, which would give her even more pleasure than seeing the old doctor.

It was decided that the doctor should stay at the inn at Dorfli and come up the mountain each day. Grandfather offered to guide the doctor to any part of the mountain that he would like to see. The doctor was delighted at this proposal. Meanwhile, the sun had been climbing up the sky, and it was now noon. Alm Uncle went indoors and soon returned with a table which he placed in front of the seat. Then he asked Heidi to lay the table and invited the doctor to join them in their simple meal.

They had golden-brown, toasted cheese, thin sliced meat, and steaming milk.

The doctor enjoyed his lunch better than he

had for a whole year past.

"Clara must certainly come up here," he said, "It would do her a great deal of good."

As he spoke, a man was seen coming up the path carrying a large package on his back. When he reached the hut, he threw it on the ground and drew in two or three good breaths of the mountain air.

"Ah, here's the package for you from Frankfurt," the doctor told Heidi. And he went up to the package and began undoing it. Heidi was filled with fresh delight as each treasure appeared. Then she ran up to the doctor and said, "Nothing has given me more pleasure than seeing you."

Then, Heidi asked him, "Would you like to come out with the goats tomorrow morning?"

"Agreed!" replied the doctor.

Heidi now went to grandmother with the box of cakes, sausage and shawl. She laid the shawl over the old woman's knees. "They are all from Clara and grandmamma," she explained to the astonished grandmother and Brigitta. "Taste how soft the cakes are!"

The grandmother could say nothing but, "Yes, yes, Heidi, I should think so! What kind people they must be!" And then she would pass her hand over the warm thick shawl and add, "This will be beautiful for the cold winter!"

Meanwhile, Brigitta stood gazing at the sausage with almost an expression of awe. She had never in her life seen such a huge sausage, and could scarcely believe her eyes.

At that moment Peter came tumbling in with the news that Uncle was coming that way. And when he saw the sausage, his eyes became as big as saucers.

Heidi understood that her grandfather had come for her and so she said goodnight to everyone and went outside. Then she and her grandfather started climbing up the mountain, towards their little hut.

The next morning, the doctor came up from Dorfli with Peter and the goats. He tried to talk to the boy, but Peter hardly spoke until they reached the hut where Heidi was waiting for them.

"Are you coming today?" Peter asked her.

"Of course I am," said Heidi. "And the doctor is too!"

Grandfather gave Peter the lunch bag, which was heavier than usual, for he had added some meat for the doctor's lunch.

Peter grinned, for he felt sure there was something more than usual in it. Then all began climbing. Heidi talked happily about the goats, the flowers, the rocks and the birds as she and the doctor climbed up the slope hand in hand. Peter sent several unfriendly glances at the doctor, but the doctor did not notice them. They reached Heidi's favorite spot and the doctor sat beside her on the warm grass. The snowfield sparkled in the autumn sunlight and the rocky peaks stood high against the dark sky.

The doctor sat silently, looking around him. A peaceful feeling came over him as he breathed the fresh air and felt the soft breeze on his face. Everything was so beautiful!

Peter, meanwhile, was feeling cross. It had been several days since Heidi had come up the mountain with him; and now, she sat the whole time beside the old gentleman. Peter could not get a word out of her.

"It is lunch time," he said after a while.

But the doctor and Heidi only wanted milk to drink, and so Peter had all the meat and cheese to himself. This made him feel much more kindly towards the doctor.

Heidi and the doctor talked for a long time. At last, the doctor said that it was time for him to go back. Heidi insisted on accompanying him as far as the grandfather's hut. After that, the doctor continued his descent alone, turning now and again to look back. Each time, he saw

Heidi standing and waving her hand to him, just like the way his own dear little daughter had watched him.

It was a bright, sunny autumn month, and the doctor came up the mountain every day. Sometimes, grandfather went with him to the higher slopes and the two enjoyed each other's company very much. Then, September came to an end, and it was time for the doctor to return to Frankfurt.

He was very sad because the mountain had begun to feel like home to him.

"I've learned how to be happy once more," he told Heidi and her grandfather.

That winter, grandfather kept his promise. As soon as the first snow began to fall, he shut up the little hut on the mountain, and went down to Dorfli with Heidi and the goats. He rented an old house near the church which had been empty for a long time. It was badly in need of repair and grandfather spent most of his time that winter making it warm and dry. Heidi went to school in Dorfli every morning and afternoon. She was eager to learn all that was taught to her.

And when the snow became hard, she was able to go up to Peter's cottage and see grandmother who was not very well and had to stay in bed.

"It's only because the frost has gotten into my bones," she told Heidi.

She was wearing a shawl to keep her warm, and Heidi noticed that her bedclothes were not very thick.

"Your bed isn't right," said Heidi. "Your feet are higher than your head."

"I know," Peter's grandmother moved her thin pillow to make herself more comfortable.

"If only I had asked Clara to let me take away my Frankfurt bed," said Heidi. "I had three large pillows there."

"Never mind," said grandmother. "I'm luckier than many sick people, and I should be grateful. Will you read me something today, Heidi?"

So Heidi read some hymns and saw how happy it made the old lady.

"Peter," she told him next day, "you must learn to read."

"I can't," said Peter.

"I'll soon teach you. Then you can read one or two hymns to grandmother every day."

However, Heidi soon came to know that teaching Peter to read was hard work. He didn't want to learn and Heidi had to threaten him with all sorts of things. She even told him he would be sent away to a school in Frankfurt if he didn't try to learn.

"I used to see the boys going there, all dressed in black," she told him.

Peter shuddered at the thought of being sent to a place where you had to wear black clothes and where they forced you to learn things. He tried harder, and eventually learned how to read. One evening, he came into the cottage and said, "I can do it now."

"Do what, Peter?" said his mother.

"Read," he answered.

Peter fetched the book of hymns and read to his grandmother.

"Who would have thought it possible?" said Peter's mother, full of amazement.

At school the next day, when Peter read from this book without the slightest hesitation, the teacher stared at him in astonishment.

"How has this miracle come about?" he said.

"It was Heidi," said Peter.

Every evening, Peter read to his grandmother, and although she was grateful, she secretly longed for spring to arrive when Heidi would come and read to her again. For whenever Peter came to a difficult word, he left it out!

CHAPTER 15

Meeting old friends

It was the month of May, and clear, warm sunshine lay upon the mountain. The last of the snows had melted and already many of the flowers were springing up through the grass. Heidi was so pleased to be back that she ran round and round grandfather's hut singing, "On the mountain! On the mountain!"

From the shed at the back, came the sound

of sawing and chopping. Heidi jumped up and ran to see what grandfather was doing. There, in front of the shed door stood a finished new chair, and a second was in course of construction.

"Oh, I know what these are for," exclaimed Heidi, happily. "This one is for grandmamma, and the one you are now making is for Clara, and then," continued Heidi, hesitantly, "or do you think that perhaps Fraulein Rottenmeier will not come with them?"

"Well, I don't know," replied grandfather. "But it will be safer to make one, so that if she comes we can offer her a seat."

Heidi looked thoughtfully at the plain wooden chair without arms, trying to imagine Fraulein Rottenmeier sitting on it!

Suddenly, there was a sound of shrill whistle and Peter appeared carrying a letter for Heidi. Heidi read the address carefully; then she ran back to the shed holding out her letter to her grandfather.

"It's from Clara!" she exclaimed, and began to read the letter aloud.

"Dearest Heidi,

Everything is packed and we shall start now in two or three days. Papa is not coming with us as he has first to go to Paris. The doctor comes every day, and is most impatient about our going. You cannot think how much he enjoyed himself when he was with you! 'No one can help getting well up there,' he often tells me. He himself is quite a different man since his visit, and looks quite young again and happy. Oh, how I am looking forward to being with you on the mountain, and meeting Peter and the goats.

I shall have first to remain at Ragatz for six weeks for my treatment, and then we shall move up to Dorfli. Every fine day, I shall be carried up the mountain in my chair and spend the day with you. Grandmamma is coming with me. But Fraulein Rottenmeier refuses to come with us. Sebastian gave her such a frightful description of the mountains, that she has become quite terrified. So, grandmamma and I will be alone.

I can hardly bear waiting till I see you again. Good-bye, dearest Heidi.

Your affectionate friend,

Clara."

As soon as Heidi had finished reading the le 'er, Peter rushed out, twirling his stick in the air in such a wild manner that frightened the goa s. The prospect of the arrival of the Frar kfurt visitors filled him with exasperation.

On the other hand, Heidi was so full of joy that she decided to go down to grandmother as soon as possible and tell her the wonderful news.

So May passed, and everything grew greener and greener. And then came the month of June that brought the flowers out all over the mountain.

This month too was drawing to its close, when one day Heidi saw a strange procession making its way up the mountain. In front were two men carrying a sedan chair, with a young girl sitting in it. Then there was a horse carrying a stately looking lady who was talking to the guide behind her. After this, came a wheelchair, pushed by another man, and then a porter carrying a bundle of cloaks, shawls and furs.

"Here they come!" shouted Heidi, jumping with joy.

As the figures came nearer, Heidi rushed forward. The children hugged each other, while Frau Sesemann was welcomed by grandfather. Then the men and the horse went back down the mountain.

"Isn't it lovely here, Clara?" said Frau Sesemann, looking all around.

Clara had never seen anything so beautiful.

"I'd like to stay here forever!" she said.

"I think the little daughter will be more

comfortable in her usual chair; the traveling sedan is rather hard," said grandfather, and he lifted the child in his strong arms and laid her gently down on her own couch. He then covered her over carefully and arranged her feet on the soft cushion, as if he had never done anything else all his life.

After this, Heidi pushed Clara round to the back of the hut to look at the fir trees. Then she showed her the goat shed, although there was nothing much to see there. The goats were out with Peter.

"I wish I could see Peter and all the goats," sighed Clara, "but we'll have to leave before then."

"Let's just enjoy all the beautiful things we can see, Clara," said grandmamma.

"Oh, look at those bushes of red flowers," said Clara.

"If you could come up higher to where the goats are feeding, you would see ever so many more," said Heidi. "And everything looks and smells so lovely up there."

"Grandmamma, do you think I could get up there?" said Clara.

"I'm sure I could push the chair up," said Heidi.

Meanwhile, grandfather had put the table and some extra chairs outside, so that they could eat their lunch in the fresh air.

The milk and cheese were soon ready, and they sat down for their mid-day meal.

"I never enjoyed anything as much as this. It is really superb!" cried grandmamma.

Clara too ate heartily, much to grandmamma's surprise and pleasure.

"It's the mountain air that gives you an appetite," said grandfather.

The afternoon went on and Frau Sesemann and grandfather talked together like old friends. Then Frau Sesemann looked towards the west and said, "We must soon get ready to go, Clara.

The sun is almost down and the men will be back with the horse and the sedan."

Clara's face fell.

"Oh, just another hour, grandmamma," she begged. "We haven't seen inside the hut yet."

The wheelchair was too wide for the door of the hut, so grandfather carried Clara inside. She thought that Heidi's bedroom in the hayloft was delightful.

"If you'd agree to it," grandfather said to Frau Sesemann, "your granddaughter could stay with us. I'm sure she would grow stronger."

Clara and Heidi were so overjoyed by this suggestion that grandmamma agreed with a smile, and it was decided that Clara should stay for a month.

Later, after grandmamma had gone, Peter came down the mountain with the goats. The animals quickly flocked around Heidi, who introduced Clara to them. Peter stood sulkily to one side and did not answer when the two girls called out, "Good evening, Peter."

Instead, he swung his stick in the air and marched down the mountain.

That night, as the girls sat in their hayloft beds, Clara looked out of the open window at the clusters of stars in the sky. She hardly ever saw a star in Frankfurt as the curtains were always closed before they came out. Now, Clara stared up at them until her eyes closed and she fell asleep.

The sun was shedding its first golden rays over the hut when Clara opened her eyes and looked with wonder all about her. She could not at first make out where she was. Then she heard grandfather's cheery voice asking her if she had slept well. She assured him that she had slept peacefully throughout the night.

Soon, Heidi awoke and was surprised to see Clara already dressed and in the grandfather's arms, ready to be carried down. She immediately got up, dressed herself in a twinkling, and ran out of the hut. There, another surprise was awaiting her: Grandfather had worked all the night and had made the door of their hut large enough to admit Clara's chair.

Meanwhile, grandfather appeared bringing two small foaming bowls of milk. Clara had never tasted goat's milk before. But when she saw Heidi drinking hers up, she did the same - and found it delicious!

"Tomorrow, you can drink two bowls," said grandfather, smiling.

When Peter came with the goats, he called to Heidi. "Are you coming?"

"I can't," she said. "I have to stay here while Clara is with me. But grandfather has promised to take us both up the mountain one day."

Peter just scowled at Clara and walked on.

The girls ate their meals outside again. As they sat under the fir trees, they exchanged news of all that had happened to them since Heidi had left Frankfurt. The day passed quickly, and all at once it was evening. Peter too came back with the goats.

"Good night, Peter," they called to him, but he did not answer.

Each day, Clara sat in the sun, ate all her food and drank all her milk, and each night, she stared at the stars and slept more soundly than ever before. She was growing stronger and healthier all the time. One day, grandfather said to her, "Won't the little daughter try and stand for a minute or two?"

And Clara made the effort to please him, although her feet hurt when they touched the ground. But each day following this, she tried to stand a little longer.

The sun shone brilliantly every day of that summer. And when evening came, the crimson light fell on the mountain peaks and on the great snowfield, until the sun sank in a sea of golden flame.

"Grandfather, will you take us out with the goats tomorrow?" Heidi asked one evening. "It's so lovely up there now."

"Very well," he answered. "But Clara must do her best to stand on her feet again this evening."

Heidi told this to Peter when he came back with the goats.

"We'll all come with you tomorrow," she said.

But Peter just grumbled some reply and swung his stick angrily in the air.

CHAPTER 16

Peter and the Wheelchair

Grandfather went out early the next morning to see what sort of day it was going to be. There was a light breeze, but the sun was on its way. Then, he wheeled the chair out of the shed, and went in to call the children.

Peter arrived at that moment. He was in a bad mood. Even the goats seemed to sense this and were keeping away from him. For weeks now, Peter had not had Heidi all to himself as he used to, as each morning she was with the invalid child on the wheelchair.

As Peter noticed the wheelchair kept outside, he glared at it as if it was an enemy. Then he looked around. There was no sound anywhere and no one was there to see him. He sprang forward like a wild animal, caught hold of the chair, and gave it a violent push.

The chair ran forward and disappeared over the edge of the slope. Down it went, faster and faster, turning head over heels several times, until finally it was smashed to pieces on the rocks.

Peter laughed and jumped for joy. Now Heidi's friend would have to go away because she had no means of getting about. And when she was gone, he would have Heidi to himself.

Soon after, Heidi came running out of the hut and went round the shed. Grandfather was behind with Clara in his arms. Heidi looked in the shed for the chair.

"Where's the wheelchair, Heidi?" asked grandfather.

"I can't find it," said Heidi. "I thought you said it was standing outside."

Just then the wind blew the door shut.

"The wind must have blown it away!" said Heidi. "Oh, if it has blown all the way to Dorfli, we'll never get it back in time to go up the mountain!"

"If it has rolled that far, it will be in a hundred pieces by now," said grandfather. "But it's a strange thing to have happened."

Clara was very upset at the incident.

"I'll have to go home if I have no chair," she cried.

Grandfather tried to calm her.

"I'll carry you up the mountain," he said. "Later on, we'll see what can be done."

When they reached the spot where the goats usually pastured, Peter was already there.

"Have you seen anything of the chair?" grandfather asked him.

"Of what chair?" said Peter.

Grandfather said no more. He spread some shawls on the grass and put Clara down on them.

"Oh, this is lovely! Lovely!" she cried, looking around.

Grandfather said he would come and fetch the children that evening, and went off down the mountain again.

The sky was dark blue and there was not a cloud to be seen. The great snowfield overhead sparkled as if set with thousands and thousands of gold and silver stars. The goats had become used to Clara and several of them came across to rub their heads against her shoulder.

Heidi left Clara with the goats for a short while, and wandered higher, where the flowers were thick under her feet and where they smelled sweetest. She breathed in the delicious scent and then ran back to Clara.

"You must come!" she said. "It's more beautiful than you can imagine. I'm sure I could carry you."

"But Heidi, you're smaller than I am!" said Clara. "Oh, if only I could walk!"

Then Heidi had an idea.

"Peter!" she called. "Come here!"

"No!" shouted Peter.

"If you don't, I'll do something you don't like," Heidi told him.

Peter was suddenly afraid that Heidi might know something about the wheelchair and was threatening to tell her grandfather.

"I am coming," he said quickly, and went down to the two girls. Heidi told him to take hold of Clara under her arms and then she did the same the other side. Together, they lifted her. Then Clara put one arm around Heidi's shoulder and the other through Peter's arm.

"Put your foot down firmly," Heidi told Clara. "I'm sure it won't hurt so much after that." And she was right. Slowly, Clara put one foot in front of the other and moved across the grass.

"I can do it!" she cried. "Look, I can take proper steps."

"Yes," shouted Heidi. "You're walking, Clara. You're walking!"

After a while, they reached the field of flowers and sat down. The flowers waved to and fro in the soft breeze and their sweet scent filled the air. Clara was almost overcome with happiness. Meanwhile, Peter lay on the ground and fell asleep, but his dreams were full of wheelchairs! He woke up sweating. And when it was time to take Clara back to where grandfather would meet them, he didn't complain once. All three were hungry, but only Heidi and Clara ate their dinners and drank their milk with enjoyment. Peter's appetite was spoiled by the worry of what was going to happen about the wheelchair.

When grandfather came to fetch them, Heidi rushed to tell him the good news about Clara.

"So we made the effort and won the day!" grandfather said to Clara, smiling. Then he lifted her up and supported her, and she walked even more confidently then before.

When Peter got to Dorfli that evening, he found people talking about the wheelchair.

"I can't think how such an accident could have happened," said a man.

"Alm Uncle said the wind might have done it," said a woman.

"No doubt the gentleman from Frankfurt will want to know what happened," said the man. Peter crept away and then ran home as fast as he could. He was certain that any day a policeman would come from Frankfurt and he would be put in prison.

CHAPTER 17

Surprises

The following days were some of the happiest that Clara had spent on the mountain. She awoke each morning, thinking, "I am well now! I can walk by myself like other people!" After several days of trying, she could now walk on her own and every day was able to walk a little further.

Then it was time for grandmamma's second

visit. The children began to prepare for Frau Sesemann's arrival. Heidi tidied the hut, and then the two girls dressed themselves and went to sit on the seat outside to wait for her. Grandfather too joined them, holding some blue flowers which he had gathered from the mountain side.

At last, Frau Sesemann's procession came up the slope.

Frau Sesemann had no sooner got off the horse, when she said, "Clara! Why aren't you in your chair?"

Then she looked more closely. "Is it really you, Clara? Your cheeks have grown quite round and rosy. I should hardly have known you."

As grandmamma was walking towards them, both Heidi and Clara stood up. Then Clara put a hand on Heidi's shoulder and the two girls began walking along quite easily and naturally. Grandmamma could hardly believe it! Laughing and crying at the same time, she hurried forward and hugged both of them in turn. Then she turned to grandfather, who was smiling. "How much we have to thank you for!" she said to him warmly.

"And God's good sun and mountain air," he said.

"And the delicious milk I've been drinking," added Clara.

"Now I must immediately telegraph my son in Paris, and tell him he must come here at once," said grandmamma.

Hearing this, Uncle went aside and whistled loudly for Peter. Soon, Peter came running down in answer, looking as white as a ghost. He quite thought Uncle was sending for him to hand him over to the police! But he was only given a written paper with instructions to take it down at once to the post-office at Dorfli.

Peter went off with the paper in his hand, feeling a bit relieved, as no policeman had yet arrived.

Meanwhile, at the very moment Peter was coming down the mountain with the telegram message, Herr Sesemann was climbing up the mountain to see his daughter.

"Is this the way to the hut where the old man and Heidi live?" he asked the boy whom he met on the way. But Peter just ran on with a frightened cry and fell head over heels, rolling and bumping down the slope. The telegram message was torn to pieces and blew away.

"How strange these mountain people are," thought Herr Sesemann as he climbed on towards the hut.

Peter rolled on down, so afraid that he barely noticed the bumps and bruises to his body. He was sure that the stranger who had asked the way was the policeman from Frankfurt.

At last he came to a halt when he was caught up in a bush. He lay still for several seconds, catching his breath. He would have liked to go home and creep into bed, but he had left the goats on the mountain and Alm Uncle had told him to hurry back to them. So he pulled himself to his feet and began to climb.

Herr Sesemann was almost there. He could see the hut ahead of him and in another minute or two would be surprising his daughter with his arrival. But the people above had seen him coming, and they were preparing their own surprise for him.

As he came closer to the hut, two figures came towards him. One of them was a tall girl with fair hair and pink cheeks. She was leaning on Heidi, whose eyes were dancing with joy. Herr Sesemann stopped and stared at the two children. Suddenly, there were tears in his eyes. The fair-haired girl looked so like Clara's mother!

"Don't you know me, Papa?" Clara

called to him.

Then Herr Sesemann ran to his child and took her in his arms. "How is this possible? Is it true what I see? Are you really my little Clara?"

Frau Sesemann came forward.

"What do you say now, dear son?" she said. "You have given us a pleasant surprise, but we have given you an even bigger one. But you must come and pay your respects to Heidi's grandfather, who has been such a help to Clara."

"Yes, indeed," said Herr Sesemann. "And here is dear little Heidi! It's a pleasure to see you." A minute later, he and grandfather were shaking hands and Herr Sesemann was pressing his heartfelt thanks to the old man.

Meanwhile, grandmamma had gone behind the hut to take a look at the fir trees. There, under the trees, she noticed a great bush of the most wonderful dark blue gentians.

"What a lovely sight!" she exclaimed. "Heidi,

dearest child, come here! Is it you who have prepared this pleasure for me?"

The children ran up.

"No, no, I did not put them there," said Heidi, "but I know who did."

At this moment, there was a slight rustling in the bushes as Peter arrived. He had tried to slip by without being seen, but Frau Sesemann called him across. Heidi had not told her who had picked the blue flowers for her and she wondered if Peter had. She wanted to thank him, but he seemed reluctant to come over.

"Come along, boy," she said. "Don't be afraid. Tell me, was it you who did it?"

Peter was looking at the ground and did not see Frau Sesemann pointing at the bunch of blue flowers. He knew that grandfather was now watching him closely, with the stranger from Frankfurt - the policeman - by his side.

Shaking all over, Peter said, "Yes," very quietly

"Well, what is so dreadful about that?" said Frau Sesemann.

"Because it's broken to pieces and nobody can put it back together again," mumbled Peter.

"Is the boy a little out of his mind?" she asked grandfather.

"No," said grandfather, who had suspected the true reason for the accident with the wheelchair from the beginning. "He was the 'wind' that sent the wheelchair down the slope and he's waiting for his punishment."

"Oh!" said Frau Sesemann. "But we won't punish the poor boy any more. Let's be fair. He was angry when we all came here and began to take Heidi away from him - or that was how he saw it. We all do foolish things when we're angry."

She went across to Peter and said to him. "What you did was very wrong, as you now know. But things have turned out for the best. When Clara had no chair to ride in, she made the effort to walk and every day since then she's been walking better and better. Now I'd like you to have something as a pleasant reminder of the visitors from Frankfurt. What would you like as a present?"

Peter was astonished. He had expected something dreadful to happen to him, and now he was being offered a present! What should he have?

"A penny," he decided after much thought.

Frau Sesemann could not help laughing. "Come here then." And she put a pile of pennies into his hand.

"I've given you as many pennies as there are weeks in the year," she explained. "Every Sunday you can take a penny out to spend."

Peter looked at the money and said, "Thank you!" Then he ran off up the mountain, jumping for joy.

Herr Sesemann turned to grandfather. "I'm a rich man, but money couldn't buy the thing I wanted most - my daughter's health. But you've made her strong. I can never really repay you for that, but I want to give you something. Please tell me, what can I give you?"

"I have enough for the child and myself for as long as I live," said grandfather. "But I'm growing old and shan't be here much longer. The child has no relations, except for one person who cannot be trusted. If I was sure that Heidi will never have to earn her living among strangers, I would be satisfied."

"I look upon Heidi as if she were my own daughter," Herr Sesemann told him. "And I promise to protect her always. And the doctor is winding up his affairs in Frankfurt, and plans to settle in this neighborhood. So, Heidi will have two protectors."

Then he turned to Heidi. "Now tell me, is there anything you wish for?"

"Yes, there is," said Heidi. "I'd like my Frankfurt bed for Peter's grandmother!"

"I'll send a telegram to Fraulein Rottenmeier," said Herr Sesemann. "The bed will be here the day after tomorrow!"

Heidi jumped for joy on hearing this, and wanted to at once rush down to grandmother to give her the good news.

"Let us all go down to her together," said grandmamma.

Then she and Heidi along with Clara's father, and Heidi's grandfather, who carried Clara in his arms, started down the mountain for Peter's grandmother's cottage.

The next day, it was time for Clara and her father and grandmamma to return home to Frankfurt. Clara was upset at first, at the thought of having to say goodbye to Heidi and the beautiful mountain home. However, Heidi reminded her of something.

"The summer will be here soon, and then you will come here again," she said. "You will be able to walk about from the beginning. We can